"You and Drew aren't arguing anymore," Ella said. "I'm glad."

"So am I," Mandy agreed.

"Me, three," Drew added.

"So does that mean we're gonna be a fam'ly?" Hope shone in Ella's brown-eyed gaze as it slid from her mom's face to Drew's.

"It means we're going to be fr⸺," Mandy explained.

Drew h⸺ s a total failure ⸺ ndy had once be⸺ e out how to be he⸺

It was pr⸺ ⸺ o avoid too many future interactio⸺ with Ella, though. She was vulnerable, and she wanted a father. Drew had no idea how to be one.

It struck Drew then that if Ben and Bonnie hadn't been hurt, if Mandy hadn't asked him to return to the Double H, he still wouldn't know about Ella. The hot embers of feeling excluded flared anew.

Friendship with Mandy was going to be hard.

But being a father? That was impossible.

Lois Richer loves traveling, swimming and quilting, but mostly she loves writing stories that show God's boundless love for His precious children. As she says, "His love never changes or gives up. It's always waiting for me. My stories feature imperfect characters learning that love doesn't mean attaining perfection. Love is about keeping on keeping on." You can contact Lois via email, loisricher@gmail.com, or on Facebook (loisricherauthor).

Visit the Author Profile page at Harlequin.com for more titles.

Hoping for a Father

Lois Richer

LOVE INSPIRED
INSPIRATIONAL ROMANCE

LOVE INSPIRED®

INSPIRATIONAL ROMANCE

ISBN-13: 978-1-335-48808-4

Hoping for a Father

Copyright © 2020 by Lois M. Richer

This edition published by arrangement with Harlequin Books S.A.

For questions and comments about the quality of this book, please contact us at CustomerService@Harlequin.com.

Love Inspired
22 Adelaide St. West, 40th Floor
Toronto, Ontario M5H 4E3, Canada
www.Harlequin.com

Printed in U.S.A.

I will lift up mine eyes unto the hills,
from whence cometh my help.
My help cometh from the Lord,
which made heaven and earth.
He will not suffer thy foot to be moved:
he that keepeth thee will not slumber.
—*Psalm* 121:1–3

This story is for those who
can't celebrate Mother's Day or Father's Day
because they've lost their precious child.
Be still and know that God is with you, that
He hears your heart's hurting cry and waits
for you to seek Him. He will be there.

Chapter One

Finished.

Exhausted, Drew Calhoun attached the computer file of the financial analysis report for his investors' group and hit Send. With a swish, the email was gone.

Contract fulfilled.

Too bad he didn't have anyone to celebrate with.

He was about to leave his desk when he noticed the flashing light on his phone, signaling missed calls. He'd silenced the machine while he was working, and he was always working. Caller ID revealed his adoptive mother, Bonnie Halston, had tried to reach him four times in the past hour.

Worry skated up Drew's spine. Bonnie never called this late at night. Something had to be wrong. He had no time to ponder what that might be because the phone rang again.

Bonnie.

"Hey, Ma," he said, using his fondest term for her. "I'm sorry I missed your calls. I've been—"

"This is Mandy Brown, Drew."

Her voice jerked him back to the last day he'd spent on Hanging Hearts Ranch, their last time together before he left for college. He'd been so happy because Mandy had said she loved him and that she would eventually marry him.

The jagged scar on the left side of his face tingled as his brain clicked through the next two months, up to the last time she'd spoken to him. The day Mandy Brown, his best friend and the only person he'd ever loved, had dumped him.

"Drew? Are you there?" Her impatient voice snapped him back to reality.

"Yeah. Sorry." He cleared his throat. "What's up?" *Keep it casual. Pretend you didn't share those moments…*

"I'm calling about Bonnie and Ben. Actually I've been calling for—never mind." Mandy's voice lost the edginess and softened. "It's bad news, Drew. They're in the hospital, in Whitefish."

"They're *both* ill?"

When it came to his adoptive parents, the Halstons, Drew's recurring nightmare was of being orphaned as he had been when he was nine years old, of once again being swamped by loss and that awful alone feeling, like he'd never be part of a family again. That same fear was closing in now. "What's wrong with them?"

"Bonnie and Ben aren't ill." Before he could breathe a sigh of relief, Mandy spoke again. "There was a fire at the ranch, in the tack barn."

Was she, like him, remembering the hours the two of them had spent in that barn? Hours when they'd mended tack, polished saddles and cleaned pebbles from hooves while sharing their dreams for the future? Those special moments were embedded in Drew's brain because Mandy was the only person with whom he'd ever shared his innermost thoughts. Later they'd shared even more.

And then it was over and he had no idea why.

Focus.

"A fire?" Drew gulped, struggling to mentally prepare himself.

In his mind he saw his foster parents standing beneath

the big black metal sign that welcomed guests to Hanging Hearts Ranch, known locally as the Double H. Situated adjacent to Montana's Glacier National Park, the ranch had been passed down through three generations of Ben's family.

What Drew had liked best about Bonnie and Ben were their three priorities. He'd always known he and his brothers, Sam and Zac, came first with the couple. Hanging Hearts Ranch ranked second, and the animals who lived there came third.

No, make that four priorities. His foster parents loved God. Fiercely.

Not Ben and Bonnie, God. You took my parents. Don't take them, too.

"How bad?" he asked.

"Originally they were airlifted to Missoula, but they're back in Whitefish now. I'm sorry, Drew," Mandy said, her voice very quiet.

"Tell me what happened," he insisted through clenched teeth.

"You remember what Bonnie's like about her horses?"

"Of course I remember," he said, irritated that she'd imagine he'd forget a single detail about the Double H or anything else in his past. *Including Mandy?* "I lived with them for nine years."

"I know." She cleared her throat as if it was hard to speak. "When the fire broke out, three of Bonnie's favorite mares were inside the tack barn getting reshod. The farrier got one out, but I guess the others were too frightened to follow. Before anyone could stop her, Bonnie rushed in to rescue them." Her wobbling voice revealed her shaken state. "I was moving some stallions. I didn't see her go in or I would have stopped her. You have to know that, Drew."

"I know." He had no doubt Mandy would have immediately interceded.

She loved his adoptive parents, had grown up on the ranch next door and called them Auntie Bonnie and Uncle Ben since she could talk. Mandy had celebrated every milestone of her life with the couple. Drew had sometimes envied the bond between the three, a bond he'd never quite forged.

"So?" he prodded, unintentionally sounding gruff. "Bonnie was injured?"

"Yes. She got the horses out but tripped at the door. Burning timbers fell on her, scorching her face, arms and neck. She also has a broken leg." Mandy paused, then added in a ragged whisper, "She would have died if Ben hadn't rescued her."

Drew winced. His brother, Zac, said burns were the absolute worst injury he had to treat in his medical practice.

"And Ben?" He almost choked on that question.

"When he used his hands to put out the flames on Bonnie, his own clothing caught fire. He has severe burns on both his hands, his legs and his feet. Plus, he inhaled a lot of smoke." Her voice trembled and she sighed. "The doctors say both their prognoses are good, but it's going to be a long road to recovery."

Mandy paused, and Drew knew she was thinking through what she wanted to say next. He'd learned to read her silences years ago. She had always been sensitive to others' pain and empathetic to a fault, which meant she was now searching for a way to tell him the worst possible news in the kindest possible way.

"Finish it," he urged, determined to get all the facts before deciding anything.

"They have very good care, Drew. You know how folks here are. Bon and Ben are a part of Sunshine. It's their community, their town. Whitefish is just where the hospital is. The folks in Sunshine have ensured that your parents know they care."

Drew could imagine how much the inhabitants of the small town would relish a chance to pay back his parents for all the things they'd done and given to their neighbors over the years.

"Old friends from town and the church are taking turns being with them and watching over them, ensuring they have everything they need. As always, Ben and Bonnie's attitudes are positive." Mandy paused. "The thing is—I promised your parents I'd keep the Double H going."

"Shouldn't be a problem for you. Haven't you been ranch foreman ever since Ben and Bonnie went to Hawaii last year?" Drew frowned. He'd never quite understood why his parents had given Mandy the job, but since they had... He wondered why she'd become suddenly silent. "Are you there?"

"Yes. I am their foreman." Mandy sounded oddly hesitant. "And I'll continue to do my job. That's not the issue."

"So what is?" Drew was only half paying attention because his brain had begun to organize next steps.

"The issue is... I need your help."

"*My* help?" He blinked.

Mandy had always been strong, competent, independent. She had a knack for drawing people together. She prided herself on partnering with others to build success. People loved to work with her because she accomplished so much.

But in the almost seven years since Drew had left the ranch, Mandy had never once asked for *his* help. Actually, she hadn't even spoken to him since she'd announced it was over between them!

"My help..." he repeated stupidly. "With what?"

"Running Ben's outfitting business. I know ranching and cattle. I don't have the time let alone the knowledge of tracking wild animals, their customs and particular habitats. I wish I'd paid more attention, but I didn't. I don't know all the specific details that his annual bird-watching groups want to hear or the best viewpoint to see whatever animal his guests are interested in. The trail rides have always been separate from my job." She paused. "But you know what's involved, Drew."

"Hey, I—"

She didn't let him finish. "You and Ben tramped the forest constantly from the first day you came to the Double H. He showed you how to track, how to find the most secretive animal, how to translate their signs in the woods and the best time and place to observe them. Probably taught you tons more than that, too. Whenever he took someone out, you always went along."

"But that was eons ago—"

"Bonnie told me you still go out with him every time you come back," Mandy insisted. "She said you've kept up with his work, even researched some stuff for him."

"It's not the same," he argued. "Of course I'll come visit them. But taking over for Ben—no. I can't."

"His first group arrives the day after tomorrow."

"Cancel," Drew said immediately.

"No way." A hint of worry underlying Mandy's swift response made him frown.

"Why?"

"Because." She waited, huffed out a breath when he didn't speak, then quietly said, "I shouldn't be telling you their business."

"If you want my help, you'd better." Drew snapped, irritated that he was still affected by that soft catch in her voice.

"Ben just took out a loan to buy six new ATVs so he can escort larger numbers on the high country trails." Mandy spoke quickly. "He's already committed to take several groups of inner-city kids on overnight, four-wheeling treks so they can see the caves."

Drew wanted to refuse again, but Mandy didn't let him.

"There's also a school science group booked. It's a commission from the school board with a promise for more if this goes well." A smile colored her voice. "Ben's delighted. You know how long he's tried to get a school contract."

"And how determined he's been to make everyone understand their responsibility to care for God's earth," Drew agreed. "I know, but—"

She cut him off again. Drew's temper began simmering.

"Spring and summer are almost solidly booked. Canceling means Ben's reputation would suffer. It also means forfeiting the deposits." Mandy's melodic voice altered, tightened.

"Okay."

"Not okay. Without those deposits, we'll never be able to cover the ranch loans," she snapped. "Unless I sell some of Bonnie's horses, and she'd never forgive me for that."

"No, she wouldn't," he agreed slowly, mulling over news of the loans. Ben hadn't said a word. "That riding academy is Bonnie's pride and joy."

"And I need those horses to keep it going. I'm doing my best to manage here, but—" Mandy stopped abruptly, then a moment later, she admitted, "I'm afraid, Drew. They could lose the ranch if we don't make those loan payments."

Drew gulped. Lose the family inheritance, which the couple had striven so hard to grow and improve? Lose the loving, nurturing place where Ben and Bonnie had brought him and his brothers when they were hurting and had nowhere to go? Lose the place where kids and adults alike came to discover God in a new way?

His parents would be devastated. Drew couldn't fathom such a loss either.

If the years of good stewardship at Double H Ranch

ended—what then? Ben and Bonnie lived to ranch. Though they'd never actually said it, Drew had always known his foster parents hoped to pass on their legacy to him and his brothers. He had deliberately chosen to ignore their hope because it was still as unlikely for him as it had ever been. He just didn't fit in at Hanging Hearts. Especially not now, with Mandy there.

"It can't be that bad," he insisted. "A few new quads wouldn't generate that big a loan. I can front them some money to cover it. It's not a problem." Making that offer helped Drew feel better about refusing Mandy. "Cancel and tell Ben's clients he'll be back next year."

"Good idea—*if* they return," Mandy scoffed. "Ben probably didn't tell you he has a competitor. And this guy is not shy about poaching clients any way he can. Canceling Ben's clients offers him the perfect opportunity to move in." She sounded annoyed. "Also, once committed to this guy, I doubt the school board would switch back to Ben."

"But Dad's the best in the business," Drew exclaimed. Mandy's silence told him there was more. "What aren't you saying?"

"So they didn't tell you." She was probably biting her lip, hating to be the bearer of bad news, looking for a way to soften it.

The memory filled his mind, and for a moment he was transported back… No!

"Tell me what, Mandy?" he demanded.

"They bought another quarter section. The Archers are retiring. They gave Ben and Bonnie first dibs on their property. Of course your parents had to buy it," she said, her voice growing stronger, assured, more Mandy-like. "The Archers' land provides access to Hanging Hearts' entire northern section. A new neighbor might not be as agreeable about granting your parents' permission to cross it."

"Not to mention that the Archers' land has Willow Creek running through it." Drew tugged at his shirt collar as if a noose was tightening around his neck. "Ben has wanted more water access forever."

"If you can't help them out now, they could lose everything. Then what will Ben and Bonnie have for their retirement?" Mandy chided. "You know how emotionally and physically vested they are in this land and their animals. Can you honestly see them living in town, without horses and cattle, or the gardens, or the petting zoo?"

An inner voice forced Drew to face facts.

Walk away? Bonnie and Ben didn't walk away when Sam, Zac and I were orphaned after the accident, or when we were stuck in the hospital, undergoing surgeries and in pain, with nowhere to go and no one to care. They were always there for us. They offered their home, supported, challenged and loved us into rebuilding our lives.

"What do you need from me, Mandy?" Drew asked with resignation.

"Help," she said quietly. "Now. I'm stretched too thin with the ranch."

She *did* sound weary, not at all like the efficient Mandy Drew remembered, certainly not like the spirited girl with whom he'd fallen in love in high school. The one who'd repeatedly assured him that his facial scar didn't matter. The girl who insisted that no matter where he went, his search to find the place he belonged, his true home, would bring him right back to the town of Sunshine, Montana, and Hanging Hearts Ranch.

Drew *had* enjoyed growing up on the ranch. He'd loved Bonnie's riding lessons and scouring the mountains and valleys with Ben, who saw God everywhere in the rocks and rivers and animals.

But home? No, the Double H had never felt like the home he'd lost.

"I know this is short notice. I know you're consumed by work and that's why you hardly ever come visit your parents, though they miss you like crazy." The comment held a hint of condemnation. "Believe me," Mandy assured him. "I wouldn't have called if I had another option."

Wasn't that the truth? Almost seven years had passed with no word from her.

"The fire happened more than a week ago, Drew."

"What?" He frowned as he thought about it. "I was overseas, speaking at an analysts convention." Dismay filled him at the thought of Ben and Bonnie alone, in pain, waiting for him to call them.

"I figured it was something like that. Thing is, I haven't been able to reach your brothers either. Apparently Sam's on some overseas assignment reporting on something in the Middle East. He's not answering his cell phone." Mandy huffed a sigh, which immediately made Drew imagine her bangs puffing out from her forehead.

Stop thinking about her! he ordered his wayward brain.

"As usual, Zac's unreachable at his medical mission in the Mali, Africa. Or wherever it is." Irritation nipped at her words. "It's probably better if you tell them about the fire anyway. Just don't let them think they need to come rushing home. Bonnie and Ben *will* recover," she insisted fiercely.

"We three group text occasionally. My brothers aren't prompt in responding but I'll text what you've told me," he promised.

"Thanks." A pause before Mandy asked tentatively, "So, can you come home?"

"I—" Drew couldn't think of one valid reason to refuse. He had nothing urgent scheduled, and anyway, he did all his work on his computer. He could bring it with him and do his next stock market analysis in Montana, at least for a while.

Besides, he needed to see for himself how his adoptive parents were faring.

"This ranch is their life, Drew," Mandy said, her tone fiercely protective. "We can't let it fail."

We. He liked the sound of that, though given their past, he had no business working on anything with Mandy. He'd loved her once and she'd rejected him. He wasn't going to be so humiliated again.

"The staff here will help however they can, though you might not know most of them."

Drew understood that she meant to remind him he hadn't been back to the ranch since a one-day visit last Christmas, when he hadn't seen her. Or the time before. Or the time before that. It was like she faded out of the picture whenever he arrived at the Double H.

"The townsfolk will help if we need it, too," she reminded. "Everyone's very loyal to the Halstons."

"Yes, I remember how—"

"Mama?"

Drew frowned at the sound of a child's voice.

"Just let me finish my phone call, okay, honey?" Love flowed through Mandy's voice. "Sorry, Drew. My daughter sometimes gets a bit impatient."

Mandy had a *daughter?*

In the pause that followed, he had the strangest thought that she was summoning her courage. As if Mandy had ever needed to look for that.

"Come home, Drew? Please?"

The words flew out of his mouth without any conscious decision.

"As it happens, my calendar is empty till mid-June or so." He gulped. That wasn't completely true, but he *would* make this trip, and he'd do what he could with Ben's schedule. This was his chance to give back some of the love and care the Halstons had spent years showering on him. "I'll be there tomorrow."

"Are you sure?" Mandy sounded like she was afraid to believe him.

"Yes. We'll plan next steps then," he said, vowing to keep his distance. Their past was over. Totally.

"Thank you. I appreciate it." She quickly said goodbye and hung up.

Questions swirled in his mind.

When had Mandy married, had a child? More to the point, why hadn't Bonnie or Ben told him? Not that Drew had encouraged talk about Mandy. In fact, he usually cut off any and all comments about his former teen love.

So he had no business wondering about Mandy's life now. But he did.

Drew remained in place, still holding the phone, staring out his glass balcony door at New York's famous cityscape spread below. He'd bought this place because he thought it met his needs. It was going to be his home. He worked here undisturbed, analyzed to his heart's content and consulted via the internet. This was *supposed* to be his haven.

But his spartan, ultra-neat apartment now seemed more like a prison.

How strange that Drew was actually looking forward to returning to the very ranch he'd so eagerly escaped.

And to seeing Mandy again.

Mandy hung up, worry and relief vying for supremacy.

Drew was coming home. That meant she'd have help keeping the Halstons' livelihood going. That pleased her.

She'd also have to tell him the truth. The prospect of that was terrifying.

"I love you, Mama." Her daughter snuggled against her side, face upturned in sweet trust that her mother would solve whatever issues cropped up in her life. Hadn't she always?

"I love you, too, Ella." Mandy hugged the little body close in an attempt to quell her growing trepidation, fighting to cling to her resolve to not let Drew's arrival at the ranch change anything.

It didn't matter what he said or did, if he reviled her or hated her. It didn't even matter that he still held a grudge, or how much that hurt after they'd once shared such closeness. Yes, she'd loved him dearly, and it had cost all her hopes and dreams to end their relationship.

But she'd never had a choice.

That was the past. Now Mandy had made a new life for herself and Ella, thanks to Bonnie and Ben. She couldn't afford to let her childish love for Drew revive and ruin what she'd built. Nor could she let guilt over the past affect her life now. She certainly couldn't let herself become the least bit susceptible to Drew's charms.

Ella was the most important part of her life now. Ella was her future.

Drew was Mandy's past. And everything about the past was best forgotten.

Everything.

Chapter Two

The next morning, Mandy caught herself glancing in the bathroom mirror for the fifth time. As if Drew would care if her hair was a shaggy mess or her makeup nonexistent. He probably dated gorgeous, uber-smart ladies with IQs like his, who wore something much more spectacular than shabby jeans, a baggy T-shirt under a denim jacket with worn-through elbows and battered Western boots.

Anyway, it was only half past seven in the morning. Drew probably wasn't even awake yet. And why did she care anyway? Better to focus on making sure Ella finished her breakfast so Trina, Mandy's au pair and home helper, could take her daughter to school.

"I sended Auntie Bonnie a text, Mama, an' I put in lots of happy faces to make her and Uncle Ben feel more better." Perched at the kitchen island, Ella popped the last strawberry into her mouth, crunching it between a smile that, minus two front baby teeth, was no longer perfect.

"I'm sure those happy faces will make them laugh, sweetie." How Mandy adored this child. "Did you thank Trina for making your hair look so pretty? And for those barrettes?"

"Yep." Ella beamed as she jerked her head up and down. "Both."

"Good girl." Mandy brushed a hand over brown ringlets framing Ella's tanned round face and innocent brown eyes. "Soon you'll be finished kindergarten," she mused, marveling at how quickly her baby girl was growing.

"Uh-huh. An' I'm gonna be six an' have a party." Ella's dark eyes shone with excitement. Then she frowned. "Don't you have to feed Magpie and Blackie this morning, Mama?" Her daughter always worried her beloved pony and dog would starve.

"I sure do. But I need a minute to admire those barrettes. So pretty. Bye, sweetheart. Be good at school." Mandy kissed her girl's downy-soft cheek, murmured "thank you" To Trina and then, with one last wave for Ella, left her house to begin another day on the ranch.

Hanging Hearts Ranch had always felt like home to Mandy, even when she'd lived next door. She'd grown up knowing Bonnie and Ben would welcome her no matter the hour. As she strolled to the stables, she mentally praised God for the couple and the job that had rescued her and Ella.

How could Drew stay away from this place? It was a beautiful spring morning. Birdsong filled the crisp air. The sun blazed, its rays already warming the land. In the distance, Ben's newest calves tottered through the grass, bawling at their mothers to be fed. Seven colts frolicked together in another pasture, kicking up their back legs to show off.

She loved it here.

Mandy gave Blackie his usual bowl of dog food. He seemed less interested in it than usual which surprised her. She shrugged and continued on her rounds. A sense of satisfaction welled but was quickly diminished at the thought of Drew arriving today. She didn't want to think about that meeting, so she focused on her job.

Someone else fed the stock, but each morning Mandy

made it a point to check out the special mounts Bonnie used in her riding academy. The most valuable stayed overnight in the stables but had been released and were currently in the nearest paddock. Spying her, they edged near the fence, jockeying for position to obtain a carrot treat.

As she fed them, Mandy mentally noted the windows on the old log cabin that she and Ella shared desperately needed washing. The usual spring rains were late this year so everything on the Double H was covered in a thick layer of dust. Add another item to her to-do list.

Wait! She blinked at the elderly woman who stood on the far side of the riding circle, obviously waiting for someone to bring her the placid mare called Babycakes so she could begin her usual lesson.

How could I have forgotten it was her lesson day?

"Mandy, dear!" the woman called, waving a gloved hand. "Good morning. Hasn't God given us a perfect day?"

"He sure has, Miss Partridge." Mandy had hoped to spend the next hour ensuring everything would be perfect for her upcoming meeting with Drew, the first time she'd see him in almost seven years. Tamping down her impatience, she asked, "How are you, ma'am?"

"Finer than frog's hair, dear." The former librarian's faded blue eyes twinkled. "I just know I'm going to ride well today."

"Let me get saddled up and we'll start your lesson," Mandy promised.

It turned out the lady's prediction was right. Once firmly mounted, Miss Partridge rode around Bonnie's riding circuit with perfect form, moving fluidly from a walk to a trot, then to a canter and finally, into a modified gallop.

"You're doing really well," Mandy told her, dismounting her own horse to help the older woman slide free of her saddle, then handing off the reins to a waiting hand. "You'll soon be ready to go on a trail ride."

"A short one, perhaps." Miss Partridge leaned forward as if there were hordes of people crowding the paddocks around them who might overhear. She whispered, *"He's back."*

"Who?" Mandy asked, intent on ensuring her not-always-stable client was on solid footing.

"Why, that handsome Drew Calhoun, of course." The elderly spinster shuffled her red orthopedic boots in the dust, her voice a whisper. "Saw him going into the Eat Café in town when I passed it on my way out here for my ride."

"Oh?" Mandy kept her face blasé. Of course that didn't work. Pretended disinterest never stopped Miss Partridge.

"I've been praying for years that the two of you would meet again. It was so sad when—well, never mind. Today God has answered my prayer." She clasped her arthritic hands together and laid them on her heart. "I just know you'll resolve whatever went wrong. The truth will always win out."

I hope not, Mandy thought, shrinking at the secret she'd shared with no one.

"I believe God sometimes uses adversity because it makes us stronger," Miss Partridge continued. "Drew's return could be the beginning of great things for you as a couple, dear."

"We're not a—"

"Excuse me, Miss Partridge." Trina smiled at the elderly librarian before addressing Mandy. "May I please have a word with you when you're free?"

"Certainly, Trina. I'll be right there." Relieved by the interruption but trying not to show it, Mandy escorted the senior lady to her vehicle. "Good riding today," she congratulated before hastily adding, "I'm sorry, but duty calls. Please excuse me."

"Oh, certainly, dear. You go ahead and get ready for your young man." Miss Partridge chuckled as she drew her vivid orange-and-pink-flowered jacket around herself, then rearranged the fuzzy purple hat she wore on every ride. "I brought along a big mug of coffee so I can sit on that bench over there and talk to God about you and—" She winked. *"Him."*

"Uh, well, thank you. Bye now." Mandy fluttered a hand before hurrying toward the log house the Halstons had given her to live in when they'd offered her a job on the Double H eighteen months ago.

"Sorry if I interrupted, Mandy, but I know you're waiting for an important call." Trina waved off her boss's thanks as she set down a steaming pail. "While Ella's coloring a picture for the teacher, I thought I'd remind you about her concert this afternoon." She worked as she talked, dipping her cloth in a bucket of water that gave off an odor of vinegar and swiping it across the dusty windows.

"How did you know I'd added window washing to my list?" Mandy gave thanks daily for this woman's help. "And yes, I noted the concert on my phone. I'll be there," she promised. "Right after it, I have that meeting at the church."

"The ladies' salad social, right?" Trina dragged a scraper across the glass expertly, leaving nothing but a sparkle behind. "Ella and I also have plans after school. She's going to have a milkshake with her friend while I pick up that skipping rope we discussed for the school contest next week. You could give it to her tonight so she can practice."

"I don't know what I'd do without you, Trina." Mandy hugged her. "And I don't want to find out."

"No worries on that score," Trina muttered glumly. "Apparently I'll be here forever. Devin Green seems to be one of those men who can't figure out the nose on his face, let alone love." She rolled her eyes. "Except the kind he feels for those cows on the back forty."

"Maybe you have to draw him a picture like Ella does," Mandy teased before answering her phone to arrange the sale of a horse. Then she moved on to check the feed being unloaded. She'd just finished speaking with the veterinarian about a lame stallion when a sound behind her made her turn.

"Hello, Mandy." His voice hadn't changed a bit.

"Drew. You're here already." So Miss Partridge *had* seen him? Mandy fought to keep her voice even. Her pulse thrummed inside her head at her first close-up look in almost seven years at the tall, lean man with the dangerously dark eyes.

But this Drew was not Mandy's teenage love. This man didn't offer that cute lopsided smirk that revealed a hint of dry hidden humor. This man looked supremely confident, assured and truthfully, a little bored. He wore casual clothes that screamed *top designer* and custom-made boots in a soft calfskin leather. Mandy longed for such perfectly fitting footwear, even knowing they'd be useless in her rough-and-tumble job at Hanging Hearts Ranch.

Drew should have looked out of place on the dusty spread, yet he appeared perfectly comfortable, even cowboy-ish, despite dark brown rumpled hair that had been clipped by a professional who knew exactly how to enhance his cheekbones without drawing attention to the jagged scar on his cheek.

Experience, that's what Drew exuded.

"How are you?" she asked politely.

"I'm fine." His brown eyes, framed by disgustingly thick lashes, surveyed her. "You haven't aged."

Ha! How little he knew.

"You don't look any older either," she lied to cover her shaking knees while wondering what had caused that fan of tiny lines at the corners of his eyes that hadn't been there seven years ago.

Drew stood head and shoulders above her, whipcord lean and still devastatingly handsome, but for sure this was not the boy she'd loved. Mandy couldn't define exactly why she felt that way, but it wasn't only that everything she saw announced successful professional.

Perhaps it was because next to him, in her shabby clothes and less-than-elegant ponytail, she felt distinctly small town.

And defensive.

But more likely it was because she'd been dreading this meeting for seven years.

God has a plan to use what you've gone through for good, Mandy.

Bonnie's familiar words echoed inside her head. As usual, Mandy wondered *what* good could come of the awful mistakes she'd made, but she quickly choked off the negative thought and got to the point of his visit.

"About Bonnie and Ben," she began, but Drew interrupted.

"I visited them last night. Thank you for ensuring they're together in the same room," he said. "They seem to be doing as well as the doctors expect. I didn't want to tire them so I didn't stay long, but if they need anything, I'll gladly pay for it." His gaze narrowed. "No expense spared for their care, Mandy. I mean it."

"You'll have to get in line. The whole of Sunshine is determined to ensure Bonnie and Ben have everything they could want for their peace of mind and healing. Everybody loves them," she reminded.

"Yeah." Drew's lips pursed for a moment. She knew that look. He was marshaling facts in his head. "You said Ben has a group booked for tomorrow?"

"Yes, though this is one group I probably could have

canceled or perhaps rebooked with no issues. It's a boys' group from the church, and our competitor has no connection with the church."

Focus on business, not the intensity of those dark eyes, she ordered her wayward brain.

"A church group. That's a bonus. I guess." Dubious didn't begin to describe his tone.

"It is, trust me." As if he would trust her ever again when he found out… "They're good about changes or substitutions on the rides. The group is scheduled for a half-day trip to Kissing Rock, a campfire supper and a talk by their youth leader before they return."

Immediately Mandy's cheeks bloomed with heat. Did Drew remember their first embrace at Kissing Rock? Did he think she'd brought it up to remind him?

"I haven't been on a ride that long for a while." A frown darkened the cinnamon glint in his eyes. Cocoa eyes, she'd once called them.

"I'm sure you'll be fine. I'll come along this first time so no worries." Mandy said it without thinking and immediately wished she hadn't offered. Drew *would* manage and she didn't need more proximity than was already inherent in this situation. She needed time and space to formulate a way to tell him about—she blinked.

What was Ella doing?

Racing across the yard, her daughter jerked to a halt beside Mandy and grinned at her before surveying Drew from head to toe.

"Hi. I'm Ella. Are you gonna be my daddy?"

Gobsmacked.

The word perfectly described Drew's current state.

"Uh—" His brain was empty, devoid of any response for this expectant child.

Thankfully, Mandy seemed completely unfazed. She smiled as she wagged a finger at the child.

"Oh, Ella, honey, you're such a tease. This is Drew. He's Auntie Bonnie's son. He's going to help with Uncle Ben's work. You can talk to him later. Right now you better get to school with Trina. Bye. Again." Mandy swept the child into her arms.

Drew figured Mandy's grip must have been too tight or else she held on for a fraction too long because Ella quickly wiggled free.

"Bye, Mama."

"I'll see you at your concert this afternoon, okay?"

"Uh-huh." Ella giggled. "I'm gonna be the tree, 'member."

"Got it." Mandy smoothed her hair, then gave her a nudge toward a woman waiting beside a gray SUV. "Off you go."

"Love you, Mama."

"Love you, Ella," Mandy replied, tickling the little girl's neck.

Ella giggled again. "Love you, Drew."

Drew knew his mouth was hanging open, but he felt completely incapable of closing it as he watched the little girl race to the vehicle and climb inside. The driver gave Mandy a thumbs-up before the two of them left.

Mandy turned, her expression a bit wistful until she noticed him watching her. Suddenly she became all business.

"So do you want to see where the fire was?"

"Uh, yeah, I'd like to take a look. But not in these clothes. I'd better change." Still bemused, Drew bent to grasp the handle of his duffel bag.

"How did you get here?" She glanced around, obviously puzzled.

"I flew to Whitefish, then hired someone to drive me. I stopped for coffee in Sunshine, met Mac McArthur. He offered to bring me out here." Drew shrugged. "I accepted his offer and sent the hired car back to Whitefish."

"Oh." She nodded. "Nice."

"Yeah." Drew frowned. "Mac says that once the insurance company is finished their assessments, a group of neighbors will come to clean up what's left and get started on building a new tack barn. Is he right?"

"That's what I've heard. Everyone has been amazing. It's as if the entire town of Sunshine has been waiting for a chance to repay Bonnie and Ben for everything they've done for everyone else." Mandy tilted her head to one side as if she wanted to ask him something, but Drew had his own questions.

"Why did Ella say she loves me?" he asked with a frown. "She doesn't even know me."

"Oh, that's just how she is." Mandy didn't look at him.

"She says that to everyone?" he asked, dumbfounded.

"Mostly. And she means it." She tugged leather work gloves from her pocket and began pulling them on. "My daughter has a very sweet heart."

"But I'm a total stranger," he objected.

"Ella has some learning disabilities. She hasn't yet grasped that some folks aren't trustworthy, and to tell you the truth…" Now Mandy looked directly at him, her green eyes intense, her tone edgy. "I'm not all that eager to disillusion her just yet." As if that ended the discussion, she nodded toward the main house. "I'm sure you'll find Bonnie's kept your room the same as always. I'll be in the petting zoo."

"Okay." Drew watched her stride away while the questions in his head multiplied. He couldn't just let her go without answering at least one of them. "Hey, Mandy?" When she turned to face him, he said, "I never heard that you'd married. Congratulations."

"You never heard because I didn't. Excuse me." She answered her phone, checked her watch and agreed to something. Then she conferred with a couple of cowboys who wanted to know where to unload two boarding horses that had just been trucked in.

Drew noted how easily she moved from one task to the next. Nothing seemed to faze her and the staff readily accepted her authority, including several men much older than her. Bonnie and Ben had told him as much, but he hadn't quite believed it.

Seeing Mandy at work proved she knew exactly what she was doing. But then, hadn't she always?

"Oh, you're still here. Sorry," she apologized as she tucked her phone into her pocket after sending a text. "It's always crazy here first thing. Listen, Drew. A couple of issues have come up. Why don't you take it easy this morning? Have some coffee or lunch. Go check your computer. I know you want to." She grinned at his blink of surprise.

He raised his eyebrows in an unasked question.

"I may live in the sticks, but I keep up with your work in the financial world. Sort of." She checked her chiming phone again, then said absently, "I'll see you after lunch. We can talk then."

"Sure." Drew walked away bewildered by all of it, but mostly that Mandy had a daughter who apparently did not have a father, which was completely unlike Mandy who ran her life in accordance with her Biblical beliefs. Stranger yet, his foster parents—her bosses—had never said one word to him about Ella's existence.

Who was the kid's father? What kind of man left a woman to raise a child on her own?

None of your business.

Maybe not, but Drew tamped down his antipathy for this invisible guy while he walked toward the house where he and his brothers had lived after their parents died. He took the stairs two at a time and twisted the doorknob, which gave way immediately. Inside, a rush of memories assailed him.

That fragrance, lavender. It was Bonnie's favorite. A new cabinet had been affixed to the wall and was filled with trophies of all sizes. He studied each. The majority were Ben's, but there were also a number with Drew's name on them, most for first place in calf-roping. Drew had always been good at that, though he was never quite sure why.

There were several scholastic trophies he and his brothers had won. They'd all loved math and science, but Drew had thrived on the complexities of statistics. Calculating odds and figuring out percentages for achieving goals had made up his world even back then, though he'd never discovered a formula for one hundred percent roping success.

Once he'd asked Ben why.

"A little puff of wind, the horse's misstep, leaning a degree the wrong way. Human failure." Ben had gazed across the ranch's acres to the white-capped mountains for a long time before smiling at him. "Everything He created for us meshes together so perfectly. I don't know, Drew. Maybe God just likes a little unpredictability sometimes."

Ben and God. Couldn't have one without the other.

How it had hurt to see the older man lying virtually helpless in that hospital bed, bound in bandages, wincing with every move, yet absolutely confident that God would get both him and Bonnie through the long period of healing that lay ahead of them.

Drew had never cultivated that same trust in God despite the fact that he'd grown up here with Ben's constant example of steadfast trust. Neither of his brothers seemed to have the same issues that he did; neither seemed to doubt that God was in charge of their lives. In fact, Zac was a medical missionary in a dangerous area of Africa and Sam traveled to the world's most hazardous hot spots to report, which told Drew that they neither felt out of step in their world, not like he had—still did.

Fed up with fighting the same questions about God that had plagued him since the car accident that had scarred him when he was nine, Drew climbed the stairs. His room looked exactly as it had before he'd left for college, when life had seemed simple and his future brimmed with plans—and with Mandy.

Back then, he thought he'd covered every detail, calculated and considered every obstacle he would encounter on the way to his future. He and Mandy would finish college. Then he'd find a job somewhere and she'd work as a vet technician. They'd get married and in their free time, they'd travel.

He'd never calculated that three months into the dream, Mandy would end their relationship.

Determined to stop thinking about the past, Drew set his bag on the desk chair and unpacked. It took three minutes to hang his clothes in the tiny closet and fifteen minutes to set up his computer and printer.

Ben and Bonnie had internet access, of course, but it was slower than a turtle. Drew mentally repeated Bonnie's oft-cited words about patience being a virtue while he waited for the Asian markets to load. He spent a few hours checking reports. His projections had been off by a tiny fraction of a percentage. A smug feeling bubbled inside. Not bad.

Drew then changed into work clothes. He made a pot of coffee that tasted horrible and heated a small casserole from the freezer that tasted delicious. Mac and cheese, his favorite and Bonnie's specialty.

He'd just finished washing his dishes when a movement outside caught his attention. Mandy, her dark blond hair bundled on top of her head, knelt in the garden, pulling weeds in Bonnie's fertile plot, maintaining the perfect rows his Ma always insisted on. For a moment Drew felt sad. If Bonnie couldn't come home by fall, who would harvest that garden, feed the abundant lettuce leaves to the animals in the petting zoo and clean the carrots grown specially for the horses?

Mandy.

Yes, of course. And she would ensure everything was done perfectly, because whatever Mandy took on, she did with excellence. That's who she was.

Which reminded Drew of Ella. How would Mandy achieve perfection for a daughter with special needs?

None of his business. Drew didn't do kids. Ever.

Pushing aside his questions, he hurried outside.

"Want me to help you weed?" he offered, mentally shuddering at the prospect.

"No, thanks." Mandy straightened and tossed him a grin. "Bonnie would have my neck in a sling if I let you and you know it."

"That was eons ago."

"She *never* allowed you in her garden after that first time, Drew. She said you didn't have enough patience to select only the weeds and ended up pulling half her carrots." Mandy chuckled at his disgust. "You know how Bonnie is about her carrots."

"Freakishly obsessed?" Drew suggested with a scowl. "I doubt it matters to the animals if they get organic carrots or not, or whether said carrots are small or large. That they get them at all should be enough."

"You don't think those gorgeous animals are worth extra effort?" Mandy demanded, pointing to six well-groomed horses placidly munching the grass while they enjoyed the warm sunshine. She dropped the bantering tone and fixed him with a serious stare. "Everything matters, Drew."

"Because?" He'd heard the argument a hundred times

before. But he wanted to hear it again, from her, not only because he'd always liked the sound of her firm yet melodic voice as she relayed her deeply held beliefs, but mostly because he wanted to know if those beliefs had changed after all this time.

"If you want to get the best, you give the best," she said, shading her eyes so she could peer at him against the bright sunlight. "Treat others as—"

"You would like to be treated," he finished and chuckled. "Does the golden rule apply even to horses?"

"To everyone. Yes." She inspected him from his head to his feet. "You need a hat. You're not used to this strong sun. Your skin will burn if you're not careful."

"Yes, ma'am." Drew pulled an old cap out of his pocket and put it on. "I'll look around for my Stetson later," he promised. "Where's yours?"

Mandy touched her head and blinked in confusion. "I thought—"

"You still lose your hat," he said, oddly relieved to know some things about her hadn't changed, daughter or no daughter. "Good thing you have thick hair."

Tendrils of it had escaped her topknot and now curled against her prominent cheekbones. It had never mattered how disheveled Mandy was, she'd always looked beautiful to Drew. He choked off that thought and kicked at the dirt.

Being back on the ranch wasn't going to be easy.

"Come on," she said. "I'll show you the damage. Then maybe you'd better go for a ride, see what you've forgotten."

"Nothing," Drew shot back, double meaning intended.

Mandy ignored that and left the garden. He matched her energetic pace to the site of the tack barn. Was she hurrying because she wanted to get this over with? He intended to ask but was too shocked by the smattering of ashes and bits of blackened timber that lay on the ground.

"It's gone," he whispered, gaping at the remains. "All the old family saddles, all Ben's grandfather's antique tack, everything—gone."

"Tack and buildings can be replaced, Drew," Mandy said quietly. "People can't."

"I know but—" He shook his head, not quite able to process it yet. "I had no idea—there's nothing left?" He glanced at her, frowned at her negative response. "It must have been intense."

"Hot and very fast," Mandy agreed. "There wasn't even time to get a hose going. The wood was really old, remember. I guess it burned like tinder."

Shocked by the thought that his loved ones could so easily have died in this inferno, Drew was suddenly reminded of the accident that had left him and his brothers orphaned and injured.

"Why would God allow this?" he demanded angrily, only realizing after he'd said it that he'd spoken aloud. "Ben and Bonnie are good people."

"I don't know why." Mandy exhaled. "All I know is that He has our best at heart. Somehow He will work this out for good."

"Still the same old blind faith," he grumbled, not even bothering to hide his irritation.

"Still doubting God knows what He's doing." Mandy shot back. "For my whole life I've believed God is good, all the time. I'm not going to stop trusting in His wisdom because something bad happened to people I care about." Her green eyes held his. Her tone held reproach. "You must remember at least that much about me."

"I wonder if I ever really knew you at all." Drew couldn't have stopped himself from saying the words if he'd wanted to. And he didn't. It was time, way past time, to air his grievances from their past.

"Why do you say that?" Far from challenging his comment, Mandy looked hurt by it. "We shared childhood, riding and holidays on this ranch. You once proposed to me. How could you not know me, Drew?"

"The girl I knew back then was, I thought, open and honest." Why didn't he shut up? Instead, the words seemed to explode out of him. "That girl wouldn't have just ended everything without giving me some kind of explanation."

"I, uh—"

"I haven't seen or spoken to you in almost seven years, Mandy. You work for my parents, you live on their ranch, yet every time I come back, you're conveniently away. You've been avoiding me. Why?"

His temper rose when she kept her blank mask in place, and though he waited for a response, Mandy said nothing. Drew doggedly continued anyway.

"My parents obviously know about your daughter, but it took them having an accident for me to find out. I'm sure it was your idea to keep Ella a secret from me, yet I have no clue why." He saw her gaze narrow. "Come to think of it, that's probably why you never wanted to explain why you ended it. You didn't want to tell me you had a child with some other guy."

Aghast that he'd actually voiced that betraying thought, Drew finally clamped his mouth closed.

"Actually, I didn't."

He wasn't sure he'd heard her correctly, but Mandy wasn't sticking around to explain.

"I have to go to Ella's concert," she said, her tone icy. "Believe what you want about me. I don't care. All I care about is my daughter and keeping this ranch running profitably until Ben and Bonnie can take over." Her emerald eyes hardened as they met his. "Then I will leave. For good." Her voice oozed scorn. "I wouldn't want you to feel like I was pushing in on your inheritance."

"I don't want…" He was talking to air.

Mandy had jumped onto a quad Drew hadn't even realized was there and was now speeding away, leaving him standing here. Alone.

With her departure, his anger and irritation dissipated to nothing. He began walking toward the house. He'd work some more. He could always lose himself in his work.

But then he paused, remembering Ben had planned an outing for some kids tomorrow. Drew needed to do a trial ride, see if he remembered the old paths.

"Never saw Mandy so riled before," a disapproving voice said from behind him. "That woman gets along with everyone, even the orneriest old bull. What did you do?"

"I didn't do anything," Drew sputtered indignantly. He exhaled, ordered calm into his brain before turning to study a man, a slightly older ranch hand, standing in front of him. "I'm Ben's eldest son. I'm taking over for him. I haven't ridden since Christmas so I'd like to get reacquainted—"

"Mandy told me this morning. That's why I'm here. She said I'm to go with you. Name's Oliver Kent, but everyone calls me Ollie. You're Drew." He thrust out a work-roughened hand and they shook.

"Nice to meet you, Ollie. But I don't need a babysitter. Just a horse and a saddle. I've ridden that route a hundred—what?" he demanded irritably when Ollie shook his head.

"Ben recently changed up all the routes," Ollie explained. "Everything works in a set pattern now. The best vista stops, most advantageous picnic spots, sites where open campfires don't pose a danger to the environment." He tilted his head just the slightest to eye Drew from under the brim of his well-worn Stetson. "Mandy told me to show you."

It was clear to Drew that what Mandy ordered happened. No point in involving Ollie in their differences.

"Okay. Let's go saddle up," he said with a shrug.

"You got any boots?" Ollie's wrinkled nose expressed exactly what he thought of Drew's fancy footwear.

"I'll check in the house. Maybe I can find my old ones." He stepped forward, then halted. "Which horse am I riding?"

"Raven." Ollie raised one eyebrow when Drew issued a snort of disgust.

"Raven's a hundred years old," he protested.

"Mandy said."

"Right." Drew strode toward the house, fuming at the indignity. If he had a vehicle handy, he'd have left.

Which would solve nothing because clearly Mandy's word was law, despite the fact that he had just as much experience on this ranch as she did.

Not true and not recently, Drew, his reasonable brain reminded. *And you're not here for Mandy. You're here for Bonnie and Ben.*

But that didn't mean he and Mandy weren't going to have another heart-to-heart. Soon.

Chapter Three

Mandy sat on her front step later that evening, phone in hand, watching the stars come out as she talked.

"Don't be silly, Aunt Bonnie. I'm glad you called. I know you're worried about your animals and your home."

"I'm more worried about how you and Drew are getting along," the older woman murmured. "I've been praying for both of you."

"Thank you. We certainly need it." Mandy held a private debate with herself before admitting, "I'm trying. But whether he's doing it on purpose or not, he gets under my skin. He's changed so much."

"So have you. It's part of growing up, sweetheart. And you're both bound to hit a few speed bumps after so many years without speaking to each other." Bonnie talked to someone else for a moment, then returned to the conversation. "Things have changed for both of you. I can't imagine Drew *wants* to be there."

"Why do you say that? This is his home. You've always made it welcoming for him," Mandy insisted, staunchly supportive of this woman who always gave from her heart. "And of course, he loved seeing you and Ben again yesterday."

"Yes, but Drew has a love-hate relationship with the

Double H. Always has." Something between a laugh and a gasp transmitted over the line.

"Are you all right?' Mandy hated that Whitefish was too far away to visit the couple after work. "Anything I can do?"

"Thank you, dear, but no." Bonnie squeezed out a breath. "It's something that only time and God can heal. But you do understand what I mean about Drew, don't you?"

"That he always compared the Double H to the home he lost when his birth parents died?" She nodded before remembering that Bonnie couldn't see. "I know he thought that. I never understood why."

"Drew's older, the big brother," Bonnie mused. "He always tried to take care of the other boys, but there was so much about their new life on the ranch that he couldn't control." She paused.

"Meaning?" Mandy pressed.

"Well, I always had this sense that Drew needed to replace what he'd lost. Or maybe he felt responsible for the accident. Maybe the three boys were arguing or something and his dad was distracted?" She sighed. "I don't know. I only know that in his nine-year-old mind, our home never measured up to the one he lost."

"And you think he's still hanging on to that? But he's an adult. He has to know differently now." It irritated Mandy that this wonderful woman should feel she hadn't given enough, hadn't done enough for Drew.

"Kids always remember the past with rose-colored glasses." Bonnie brushed it off as if it didn't bother her, but Mandy knew better.

"The other Calhoun brothers loved it here."

"Not enough to come back and stay," Bonnie pointed out sadly.

"No." Mandy hesitated but finally confided, "In high

school I always felt that Drew loved the ranch and everything on it."

"Really?" Bonnie sounded skeptical.

"Yes. He took great pride in naming the Double H as his home when he won all those roping contests." Mandy so wanted to ease this adoptive mother's heart.

"Yet he never mentioned staying on the ranch or taking over." Bonnie's words held regret. "He was always college-bound."

"I think Drew *did* want to stay. I think that inside he was torn about leaving." It sounded silly, but Mandy couldn't rid herself of the feeling that had persisted since high school. "I've always wondered if that was because he was afraid of taking over, afraid of the responsibility, afraid of failing."

"Drew? Failing?" Bonnie scoffed in a gentle chuckle. "It's nice of you to make me feel better, sweetie, but I always knew Drew was focused first and foremost on his math studies. It's only natural he felt compelled to see where his interest would take him."

Mandy let that go, uncertain about asking what was on her heart.

"What are you thinking, dear?" Bonnie had always been able to read her silences.

"What I said about him being afraid…" She bit her lip, but the question wouldn't go away.

"Yes?" Bonnie prodded.

"Do you think fear could have been behind Drew's insistence that he never wanted kids?" When Bonnie didn't immediately respond, Mandy hurried on with her thought. "We never discussed it, you know. I think it was a foregone conclusion with him, that he assumed I felt the same."

"Maybe because having a family didn't fit into his excessively meticulous plans," Bonnie murmured. "Remember those lists for your futures? He tried so hard to predict every detail of life, as if anyone can do that." Her chuckle was quickly followed by a gasp. "Note to self, don't laugh again. It hurts."

Immediately guilt filled Mandy. Why was she bothering Bonnie with this?

"Sorry, sweetie," Bonnie said gently. "But I can't explain Drew's reason for not wanting children in his world."

"He really stressed it on the phone that time, right before I was supposed to come home for the break in October. That was the weekend I was going to tell him—" A new thought hit. "Do you think Drew knew I was pregnant?"

"How could I possibly have known that?"

Mandy gasped. Drew stood at the bottom of the steps, staring at her, eyes dark with confusion and—anger?

"I have to go, Bonnie," Mandy said into her phone as her heart sank to her toes.

God, this is so not the way...

"I'll be praying, sweetie." Bonnie hung up.

Mandy tucked her phone into her pocket as she tried to figure out how to do this without hurting Drew.

But there was no way.

"Mandy?" Uncertainty, though it would be barely perceptible to anyone who hadn't known him as she had, laced the edges of Drew's voice. "Why in the world would you imagine I could've known you...?"

He stopped, froze, and then reared back as if she'd struck him with a two-by-four. His eyes searched hers as his brain began assembling the pieces.

"Ella—" Drew seemed to choke on the name.

"Is your daughter." Mandy was amazed at the weight that fell away when she finally said it. But that was quickly replaced by panic as he towered over her, eyes burning. "I intended to tell you that weekend," she whispered. "But then you called, furious because some kid had spilled his soda on your computer and you'd lost your entire project and it was his fault and…"

He said nothing, merely crossed his arms and waited for her to explain.

"You were adamant when you said you never wanted children, Drew. You said you couldn't imagine ever being tied down. You said you had a lot to do with your life and children weren't going to be part of it." Mandy let it all pour out, every pain-inflicting word, as well as the soul-deep ache that had almost drowned her. "I tried to reason with you, do you remember?"

"No." Drew shook his head once, his face an implacable mask.

"That weekend we were both home. I intended to tell you. I tried so hard to discuss family, children, how they could make us better, improve our world. How they're our hope for the future. I used every possible reason I could think of to get you to retract," she whispered. "I tried everything."

"Except the truth." Icicles hung off his words. "When you couldn't convince me, you went back to Missoula and concocted your pathetic little brush-off, right?" His snide smile flickered. "I knew something was up with that whole scenario. I tried to contact you, but you'd moved, changed your phone number—" He broke off, thought for a minute, then demanded, "Did Bonnie and Ben know?"

"No one knew," she said, choking back tears. "I had a little money left from selling our ranch, the bit that was left after I buried my parents and paid off their debts. I got a job and worked as much as I could until Ella was born."

"And then?" Fury seemed to radiate from Drew, and the worst part was that Mandy couldn't blame him. He had to be feeling shocked, confused, betrayed. All the things she'd felt. The difference was she'd had six years to get over it.

As if she'd ever get over losing... She pressed on.

"Ella needed ongoing specialized care for a while. It cost a lot." Mandy licked her lips, mentally cowering under the bitter thrust of his chin. "When she was four and a half, I had to take her to a heart specialist. We were coming out of the medical building when I ran into Bonnie and Ben. As soon as they saw her, they knew the truth."

"Yet no one told *me*." Hostility laced the words.

"How could I, Drew? Your words were unequivocal. You'd said repeatedly that you did not want children. At all. Ever." Though it was wrong and Mandy had regretted what happened because she'd gone against the Biblical principles she'd always held dear, Ella *had* come from love. Mandy could not, would not, regret her daughter.

"Excuses," he grated, eyes hard as onyx chips.

"You were in the midst of your master's degree by the time I met your parents, Drew. Bonnie and Ben were desperately struggling with the ranch. Don't you remember?"

Drew said nothing so Mandy continued.

"They must have thought Ella and I looked like beggars. They insisted on getting my address. That evening they took us out for dinner. Afterward, Ben took Ella to the park while Bonnie dug the truth out of me." She smiled. "Once they knew our situation, those two precious soft hearts wouldn't leave us in our shabby boardinghouse until I promised I'd still be there the next morning to go to breakfast with them."

"Why didn't they give me your phone number? I asked them for it often enough." The porch light illuminated a flickering muscle in his neck.

"I didn't have a phone, Drew. Couldn't afford one. I couldn't afford anything. I'd spent the last of our food stamps that morning on milk for Ella. I know how corny that sounds, but it's true. We were desperately poor." She gulped. "If it had turned out that Ella needed heart surgery, I had no way to pay for it."

She could read his thoughts in the glower clouding his face. *My parents could.*

Irritated by his judgment but determined not to give in to anger, Mandy pressed on, "Thank God she didn't need heart surgery."

"Oh, yes," he agreed contemptuously. "Thank God."

"The next morning Bonnie and Ben showed up with movers." Mandy ignored his scorn. "I'd been laid off. They offered me a job at the ranch, insisted they needed my help. Bonnie had hurt her back, remember? And the reason they were going to the cardiologist, the same one Ella was sent to, was because Ben was getting checked out for heart issues. Neither of them were in good shape. I couldn't refuse to help them."

None of this seemed to reach Drew, who kept glaring at her. Mandy continued with the story, desperate to get it all told now so she could escape.

"So I came back here," she said quietly. "That was a year and a half ago."

"And now you run Hanging Hearts Ranch." Drew's lips curved in a cruel smile.

"Yes, but it wasn't immediate. I've worked my way up, proven I can handle the job. It wasn't charity either," she defended hotly.

"Of course not. Because you were a rancher and you had the wealth of experience my parents needed." His nasty tone and dubious expression made her rush to explain.

"Yes," she said proudly, thrusting up her chin. "I did. You never understood or appreciated my knowledge of ranching, Drew, because you never wanted to know. You were too involved in your own interests. Truthfully, you didn't care what I knew unless you needed my help."

Drew looked ready to explode, but Mandy wasn't giving him a chance.

"When Dad got sick, I ran our spread on my own for over three years, though I doubt you or anyone else realized it," she said sadly, remembering those difficult days and how she'd wished he'd noticed how badly she was struggling. "I tried really hard to protect his pride."

"Hardly the same thing as managing the Double H," he said mockingly.

"It was exactly the same," she shot back. "How do you think I knew the best feed combination for your roping stallion, Drew? Or how to build his muscle with those exercises I insisted you practice before your contests?" Mandy would not allow him to put her down, not in this area. "Dad taught me everything he knew and that was a lot."

"That's—"

"In our senior year, when we had so much snow, who do you think advised your parents to get their herd out of that upper pasture? I did. Because I'd already moved our herd and knew yours couldn't tolerate the conditions up there for long." Mandy could see the stubbornness in his eyes but she refused to back down. "Do you remember when wolves stole other ranchers' cattle? Why do you think hungry scavengers left the calves on the Double H alone? It was because your parents changed their fencing—at my suggestion."

What was the use? She could see he didn't believe her.

"Of course you don't remember," Mandy muttered. "You never bothered with my world. You never even asked me if I wanted a family. You just assumed that I wanted the same things as you." Perhaps that was harsh, but she was fighting for her child now.

"So it's time to paint me as the bad guy," he derided.

"It's not about you being bad, Drew. It's not even about us." Frustration told her to give up, but Mandy continued anyway. "Don't you get it? It's about the truth. You don't believe me? Ask your parents what it was like when I got here with Ella."

"I'm sure they'll tell your sad—"

"The day I arrived, I noticed several cattle on the west flat that didn't look right. I isolated them immediately because I had a hunch they could have hoof-and-mouth disease." She ignored his gasp and pursed her lips, remembering that tense time. "If it infected the herd, Ben and Bonnie could have lost everything. I insisted we quarantine all our animals for six months. We couldn't sell any of them until we found out which were infected. We had to wait and see how bad it was."

"More secrets. No one told me any of this." Drew's eyes narrowed. "What did my parents do for income if they couldn't sell their animals?"

"Ben increased his outfitting, turned it into a business instead of just a hobby. Bonnie added evening riding classes and began raising chickens. She sold eggs in town." Mandy wasn't sure whether to reveal just how dire the situation had been, or to gloss it over so he wouldn't feel guilty.

"What else? I want to know it all," he insisted.

"We expanded the garden and sold every extra bit of produce we could raise at the local farmer's market," she told him. "During winter evenings and in our spare moments, Bonnie and I quilted. We sold the quilts online because your parents didn't want any of the local folks to know how bad it was."

"But why didn't they say something?" Drew challenged. "We boys could have helped out, financially if nothing else."

"They didn't want you to know and I couldn't contravene their wishes," Mandy pressed on. "We sold some of the horses. Hay was in high demand that year and we had lots so we made some good deals selling to the neighbors."

"What else?" He still looked as if he thought she was making this up.

"Lots of things. We rented ourselves to help farmers harvest their crops. I taught trick riding to anyone who would pay the fee. I sold pictures of Ella to a magazine." She shrugged. "We did whatever we could to make money to pay the bills and keep going until we finally passed all the government inspections and could sell Double H cattle again."

"No doubt making you their hero," he sneered. "Are you finished?"

"No, actually I'm not." Mandy was tired of explaining, but she wanted it all said, everything out in the open. "You challenged my ranching abilities, Drew. Well, when your dad grew more focused on his trekkers, I thinned out your parents' horse stock and sold off the aging animals for as much as I could get. Once the ranch was cleared by the inspectors, I brought in different breeds of cattle and horses to vary our offerings and get more strength. Successfully, I should say, because now people are asking to buy our cattle and our mares."

He said nothing.

"I also sacked some of the more inexperienced hands. We couldn't afford to pay them all. Later I hired new ones who didn't need me to tell them every move, guys like Oliver." She glared at him. "I think I've carried my weight here, Drew."

"And probably shoved your daughter on my parents at every opportunity." It was his annoyance at her speaking, but that didn't prevent Mandy from being infuriated.

"Ella is *your* daughter and their granddaughter!"

"So *you* say." He looked hard and implacable. How he'd changed.

"I won't sit here and let you condemn me or our child because you're angry. I did my very best for the ranch and your parents." Mandy jumped up from the doorstep. "You're so good at math, Drew. Figure it out."

She paused then, unable to walk away with this anger simmering between them, even though there was nothing about Drew's silence or foreboding expression that encouraged her to stay. They had been so close once. Of course, that was over, but they still had to work together. She had to at least try to reach out.

"I've followed your articles, read about and applauded your success," she offered quietly.

"Oh, I'm sure. You were always so into calculation." His scathing comment relit the fire inside her.

"That's your biggest problem, Drew," she snapped. "You don't think the rest of us are smart enough to have done well. You can't possibly imagine that I might excel at something." Sadness replaced her anger. "You lock yourself in your narrow box with your numbers and a webcam, and you analyze what's happening in the world. But you see only a tiny pinprick of what's really happening."

"And you see it all?" he snarled.

"No. But I do see people. I hear them and I listen to them. Parents who love you so much and worry about you. I hear them when you don't call, wondering if you're okay or if you need anything or, most of all, if you even want them in your life anymore." She felt tears well but refused to shed them in front of him. "I see how much you need them, and I see they need you, too."

"Let's get back to the point. Your daughter." His closed expression told her he'd rejected her criticism.

"Her name is Ella and she's your daughter, too. Not even you could have forgotten those last hours we spent together." Suddenly Mandy couldn't do this anymore. It besmirched the love they'd shared. "Don't worry, Drew.

I don't want or expect anything from you. You have no responsibility here. All I wanted was to finally tell you the truth."

Clearly he didn't believe her. How deeply that hurt.

"Ella is mine. I love her more than life, just as I do Bonnie and Ben. I will do whatever I have to in order to protect all of them." Mandy inhaled, then looked him straight in the eye. "Even if that means I have to work with you."

Mandy turned and walked up the stairs. Inside her little log house she closed the door, glad of the strong walls, so thick they would prevent Drew from hearing her sobs of despair.

"I promised I'd work with him, Lord. I promised for Bonnie and Ben's sake," she prayed through her tears. "But he's so hard and bitter and angry. It's going to make the next few months so painful. Please help me. And God? Please protect Ella. I don't want her to feel Drew's disparagement or negativity, though once he knows the whole truth…"

If she'd told Drew everything, he'd have left by now. And she needed him here. So for a while, she'd hang on to her secret.

Mandy got ready for bed knowing there would be little rest tonight. After checking that Ella was still sound asleep and brushing a kiss against her daughter's rosy cheek, she wrapped her fuzzy housecoat around herself and sank in her favorite chair to read David's book of Psalms, searching for comfort.

But Drew's words rode a merry-go-round in her head.

Your daughter.

Meaning he wanted nothing to do with Ella.

So much for those silly reveries of family Mandy had once fantasized. That wasn't going to happen. As Miss Partridge was fond of saying, the truth always won out.

The only question was when?

* * *

Furious, Drew paced around the darkened ranch. His own parents hadn't told him the truth. Wasn't that proof that he didn't really belong here, that this ranch wasn't and never had been his real home? And Mandy? She'd kept Ella a secret for years. She deserved his scorn.

Does that make you feel better? his brain demanded.

Drew didn't feel better. He felt outraged and betrayed and…abashed at the awful things he'd hinted at, sickened by what he'd actually *uttered.* His appalling taunts to Mandy replayed inside his head, each scornful remark stabbing him with repugnance. In the back of his mind, he heard Ben's voice.

Shame on you, son.

And Bonnie's: *That was unworthy of you, Drew.*

They'd both see his ugly behavior as a reflection on their parenting.

Repulsed by his actions and shocked by how little he'd known about the ranch and Mandy's part in helping his parents, trapped in a vortex of self-condemnation and fury, Drew walked to the woodpile. As he'd done in his youth when life grew messy and didn't fit his preplanned paradigms, he began chopping firewood.

Alone with his tortuous thoughts, Drew split logs until his arms grew weak and wobbly and his body burned hot with perspiration. When he was too exhausted to continue, he stacked the pieces under the roofed wood box and then lit a fire in the pit where he'd once shared hot dog nights and sing-alongs with his parents and brothers. And Mandy.

He sat on a hewn-log bench and peered into the flames, struggling to organize what he'd learned into some form of order.

He had a daughter. Ella.

Drew closed his eyes against the truth, not wanting to

remember the past. As if he could forget. He didn't want to think about Ella either, not her chirpy voice or how her charming ringlets danced with every move. He sure didn't want to replay her asking if he was her daddy.

Drew wanted to deny everything he'd been told. But he'd always dealt in facts. The facts were that while he'd been completely and utterly focused on himself, *his* life, *his* world and *his* future, his parents had been in a battle to save their ranch and the life they loved. Mandy, who was no relation and was already dealing with single motherhood to a special needs child, had selflessly stepped in for him and his brothers. She'd gone above and beyond.

Drew had decried her for *that*? His dislike of responsibility was no excuse. But he would do better. He was here now, and he would put his parents' needs first.

And Ella? Mandy wouldn't lie about that. Drew must be Ella's father. But the responsibility for another life was daunting. Happy, smiling Ella, with soul-deep giggles and big brown eyes that sparkled with fun. It wasn't her fault Drew was allergic to responsibility.

Yet somehow Ella had crept into his head. What did she like most about living on the Double H? What did she dislike? Did Bonnie hug her as tightly as she'd once hugged Drew? Did Ben rub his whiskers on Ella's cheek when he teased her, as he'd often done to Drew and his brothers?

What about Bonnie and Ben? Did they like being grandparents? Actually, they already were to Zac's twin girls. But his parents seldom got to see those grandchildren. Ella was right here, just across the yard.

Did Ella have any of *his* characteristics? Her hair and eyes were the same shade as his. Mandy was blond with green eyes. Ella seemed tall, like he'd been for his age. Mandy was petite. Ella strode about the ranch with the same inner confidence as her mother, something Drew had always envied. Mandy had always seemed secure in the knowledge that whatever happened, God would be there for her. Ella, too. Drew had never found that security.

The truth was, Drew had missed Mandy without even knowing it. Missed the way she ignored his pretense and forced him to face his underlying issues, as she'd done this evening. Missed her blunt honesty and her challenges to be more than he thought he could be. Missed her kindness and generous spirit.

What if she'd told him she was pregnant? Would he have been as good a father as Mandy was a mother? No. Drew feared responsibility. But he *was* just as responsible for Ella as Mandy.

He sat alone in the moonlight, watching the sparks fly upward as the truth bloomed. He owed Mandy an apology. A big one. The thought of giving it terrified him, and not only because he was deeply ashamed. Except for discussions about anything math related, he'd always struggled to express himself verbally. He never got the words quite right when important or personal matters were involved. That was why he preferred his computer. If he tried to say he was sorry to Mandy, he'd probably mess up worse than he already had.

Hard to imagine, his brain scoffed.

Bonnie's advice from eons ago clicked in his brain.

If you can't say it, Drew, write it.

Yes! He'd write Mandy a letter of apology.

He set the screen top over the diminishing fire to keep the sparks from flying away. Assured that he would not cause an incident on the bone-dry ranch, he went inside, sat down at Ben's desk and selected a plain white sheet of paper.

Then he began writing.

Dear Mandy

Dear? Drew scrunched up that paper and started again.

Mandy.
I'm sorry and I apologize. For everything. You've done an amazing job with the ranch and I know it. I was angry and shocked about Ella and I took it out on you. I shouldn't have.

It took forever to write and rewrite his admission of guilt, to ensure he expressed his honest regret and to beg her forgiveness. Hours later Drew was reasonably happy with the final result. He started the coffee maker, surprised to realize dawn had arrived. Then he realized his letter required one thing more if he truly wanted Mandy's pardon.

I promise I will do my best to work as your employee, to make the Double H run smoothly until Ben and Bonnie return.

Drew added it quickly, before he could change his mind. Satisfied, he took a gulp of coffee for courage and immediately grimaced at the awful taste. After stuffing the letter into an envelope, he sealed it and wrote Mandy's name across the front in huge letters. The moment he set it on Ben's desk, the pent-up frustration and bitterness knotted inside his gut eased.

Drew still felt he'd been betrayed by his parents and by Mandy. And he was still scared of being someone's father. What if he did something wrong? Or what if Ella found out he wasn't the daddy she wanted? What if, what if, what if? The possibilities for failure grew exponentially in his mind.

Fingers outstretched to grab the envelope and shred it to bits, Drew glanced up and saw Bonnie's painting of Jesus walking on water. Not just smiling, but laughing, ear to ear, as if he'd never had so much fun in His whole earthly life. The caption read, *Fear not*.

Bonnie would say he'd just received a sign from God.

Drew swallowed the rest of his awful coffee, picked up the envelope and walked outside, across to Mandy's house. He shoved the envelope into her doorframe and was almost back at his parents' house when he heard a child scream.

Though the sound terrified him, Drew scanned the yard until he spotted Ella crouched on the ground beside a massive black Labrador. Had she been bitten? Mauled? Fear grabbed him by the throat, but he ignored it and raced to the child.

"What's wrong? Did he bite you?" His stomach in knots, Drew searched for something he could do, something he could fix. Wasn't that what fathers were supposed to do? "Are you hurt? Tell me what's wrong, Ella."

"It's B-Blackie," she bawled, tears pouring down her cheeks. "He won't wake up." She gulped. "Is he d-died, Drew?"

Mandy should be here, dealing with this. Drew had no idea how to handle a pet's death and given he his fingertips found no heartbeat in the black fur, that's likely what had happened.

"I'm sorry, Ella, but yes, I think Blackie has, uh, died." He looked at the dog more closely, remembering his own past. "I think he must have gone to sleep here a little while ago and never woke up."

"He's been getting kind of slow. Mama said that's 'cause he's really old." She hiccupped back a sob, climbed into Drew's lap and flung her arms around his neck. "B-Blackie is my very b-bestest friend," she said, weeping against him. "I don't want him to go in the ground, Drew. He likes to run and play, not be died."

Now what? Drew slid his arm around Ella's waist because, well, what else could he do? Strangely, he didn't mind her hugging him.

Drew knew about loss. Trying to remember what Bonnie and Ben had said to comfort him when his own dog had died, Drew tentatively set his other hand on Ella's curly head and let it slide down her hair, remembering. Perhaps his touch would soothe her the way Ben's had done for him the day he'd buried his pet.

"Putting Blackie's body in the ground won't hurt him, Ella." Drew tipped her tearstained face up and smiled, hoping he looked reassuring.

"It w-won't?" Ella's frown marred her smooth forehead. Her eyes were totally trusting. "How come?"

"Because Blackie's body was...like his shell," he told her, feeling his way through the miasma of uncertainty surrounding death.

"A shell—like a turtle?" Ella's expression said she thought Drew was silly. Maybe he was. But he couldn't stop now.

"Kind of," he agreed. "You see, Blackie's body, and our bodies, too, are what we live in when we're here on earth. But when we die, we don't need them anymore."

"'Cause we're in heaven with God. That's what Auntie Bonnie told me." Ella nodded.

Auntie Bonnie. Not Grandma.

"That's right." Was it stupid to feel grateful that Mandy had left that truth unsaid to Ella?

"'Cause we'll have wings in heaven." Ella giggled.

"What's so funny?" he asked, utterly confused by this mercurial little girl.

"Blackie flying." She giggled again. When her fingertips brushed against his bristly cheek, Drew sucked in a breath, shocked by the stomach-clenching sensation her tender touch caused. "How do you know about dogs?"

"Because I used to have one. His name was Rover.

Here." Drew offered her a clean tissue from his shirt pocket and grimaced as she blew her runny nose. "When Rover died, Bonnie and Ben helped me build a box for him. He's buried in it underneath a tree."

"On the ranch?" When he nodded, Ella glanced around the yard. "Where?"

"I'll show you." Drew set her on the ground before rising. Then, with her tiny hand clasped in his, he led her to a huge cottonwood tree. Under it stood a little white cross with *Rover* painted in black.

The lettering looked freshly done. Ben or Bonnie must have recently retouched it, he decided, moved by such a kind gesture.

"I didn't know Rover was your dog. It's pretty here." Ella's hand squeezed his as she studied the daffodils flowering around the cross. "Can Blackie have a nice place like this to stay, Drew?"

"I think Rover would be okay with sharing his spot." He bit his lip for a minute, then spoke quickly, partly to stop her obviously imminent tears and partly because he felt like he had to do something. "I'm not very good at carpentry stuff, but maybe you and I could make a box for Blackie to stay in beside Rover."

"Really?" She hugged his legs so tightly Drew had to alter his stance to keep his balance. "Yes, please. And thank you," she added as if suddenly remembering she was supposed to say that.

"It's okay." He patted her head, feeling awkward, like a bull in a china shop, and suddenly desperate to escape. "Why don't I go get Blackie and lay him here on the grass to wait until his box is ready?"

"O-okay." She sniffed sadly. Then she flopped onto the ground, arms hugging her middle, just as Mandy used to do. Only Ella was humming a little tune.

Jesus loves me. He remembered the song from long

ago. Weren't there some actions that went along with those words? Lost in his past, Drew walked to the dog and lifted the bulk into his arms.

"What's going on?" Mandy appeared across from him, a worried expression marring her pretty face.

"Ella's dog died. We're going to let Blackie rest beside Rover while I figure out how to make a box for him." Drew wondered if she'd seen and read his letter, if she'd come tell him to mind his own business when it came to Ella and her dog.

Judging by the way Mandy stared at him, her freckled nose wrinkled and her mouth hanging open, she thought he'd gone insane. "A box?"

"A kind of casket. Is that okay?" Drew felt stupid, like the misfit he'd always felt he was. He suddenly wished he was anywhere else but here.

"It's—very kind of you, Drew." Mandy walked with him to Ella, who immediately jumped up, threw her arms around her mother and began a long-winded, tearful explanation. "I'm sorry, baby," Mandy consoled. "I know you loved Blackie so much."

"Like Drew loved Rover." Ella leaned her head back to stare up at her mother. "Drew's not nasty like you said. He's really nice about dogs."

Mandy's face turned a vivid red. She ducked her face, refusing to look at him.

Drew grabbed his opportunity.

"Actually, Ella, I have been nasty, rude, mean and extremely ungrateful to your mama," he murmured. "And I'm sorry. Would you mind if we started over, Mandy?" He held his breath.

"I was thinking that after I read your letter." She studied him, her gaze intense, searching, missing nothing. "Thank you for writing it."

"I meant all of it." He gulped and pressed on. "I'm back,

Mandy. I'm here to help you with whatever you need. I'll try to do it without all the drama and blame. So can we please start again?"

After a moment's hesitation, Drew thrust out his hand. To his great relief, she shook it.

"I'd like that," she said, green eyes shining clear, a smile tilting her lips. "It wasn't all your fault. I'm sorry, too."

"Let's leave it in the past." Drew exhaled, feeling somehow lighter. "Can the three of us build a box for Blackie?"

"Yep." Ella paused to glance back at her dog and sniffed. She twisted to study her mother and then Drew before bursting into a fit of giggles. "You and Drew aren't arguing anymore," she said as she slid one small hand into each of theirs. "I'm glad."

"So am I," Mandy agreed.

"Me, three," Drew added.

"So does that mean we're gonna be a fam'ly?" Hope shone in Ella's brown-eyed gaze as it slid from her mom's face to Drew's.

"It means we're going to be friends," Mandy explained, breaking the pregnant pause that had fallen.

Drew hoped she was right. He was a total failure at relationships, yet he and Mandy had once been close. Surely he could figure out how to be her friend now.

It was probably best to avoid too many future interactions with Ella though. She was vulnerable, and she wanted a father. Drew had no idea how to be one and no intention of assuming that role. Mandy didn't want that either. Once he'd done his bit to help out here, stayed until mid-June, he'd leave again.

It struck Drew then that if Ben and Bonnie hadn't been hurt, if Mandy hadn't asked him to return to the Double H, he still wouldn't know about Ella. The hot embers of feeling excluded flared anew. It took enormous strength to douse those coals and concentrate on what he was here to do.

Friendship with Mandy was going to be hard.

But being a father? That was impossible.

Chapter Four

That afternoon, Mandy surveyed the clouds in the western sky with critical eyes.

"Rain?" Drew asked from behind her.

"I don't think so." She turned to face him. "The air doesn't smell like it. Sorry."

"Why sorry?" He stared at her blankly. "You're not in charge of the weather."

"No, I'm not." *Stop bristling*, she told herself. "I was making a joke, Drew. If it rained, you wouldn't have to take the boys' group out. Ha ha." She faked a laugh, wishing this tension hanging between them would dissipate.

"You don't take groups out if it's raining?" There was curiosity in his question, nothing else.

"Sometimes we do. Never kids," she explained. "We usually plan something else."

"Oh."

Drew stood tall and lean in a pair of worn jeans that Mandy figured they had come from his former closet, since they looked about three inches too short for his long legs. The blue-and-black plaid shirt was one of Ben's, as was the black Stetson Drew wore. In fact, he looked much as he had seven years ago, just before he'd ridden in a bronc contest. Except he wasn't smiling now.

"There really isn't any need for you to come along on this ride," he said, dark eyes intense as they studied her. "I have done it before."

"I know." She stifled a remark about how long ago that had been. "And believe me, if Bailey Sanderson wasn't coming, I'd probably send you on your way with a wave. Since he is…" She shook her head and sighed. "I'm going."

"Who's Bailey Sanderson?" Drew asked as he walked with her to the paddock.

Mandy said nothing, waiting for enlightenment to dawn. Sure enough, Drew faltered midstride, then grabbed her arm.

"Not Jeff Sanderson's kid?" He almost gagged on the name of his high school nemesis.

"His eldest son, Bailey. Age eight," she confirmed with a grim nod. "I'm afraid it's like father like son."

"Does Jeff know I'm here?" he demanded, voice tight.

"I certainly didn't tell him. That man hasn't grown up one iota since high school. He still thinks he's the hottest ticket in Montana." Inwardly Mandy fumed.

"Jeff was always on my case in high school," Drew murmured. "But you got along with him. So what did he do to get your ire stirred up?"

"Asked me out." Stuffing down her disgust, she mentally chose the horses she wanted for the ride while noticing the grass was turning brown from the drought.

"I thought Jeff was married?" Drew grasped a bridle and petted one of the older horses who leaned over the fence to nudge his shoulder. When Mandy didn't respond, he stopped, glanced at her face and grimaced. "Oh."

"That's all you have to say?" She unclenched her jaw. "I've tried to be nice to Jeff because Sheena is my friend and she loves him. I was her bridesmaid at their wedding. But now she's bedridden with their third child. How dare Jeff ask me out?"

"Maybe he just wants someone to talk to." He winced
t her glower. "Okay, that was stupid. If he's the same as
e was in high school, I'm sure he has a ton of buddies he
ould talk to."

"Or his wife," she said pointedly.

"True." Drew frowned. "Can't figure out why he'd hit
n you. In school you always called his bluff. He should
now you wouldn't let him get away with misbehaving."

"Misbehaving? That's what you call it?" she demanded
ngrily.

"I was trying to be nice. Want me to talk to him for
ou?"

"No!" Mandy exploded. "You're not my keeper, Drew.
Besides, the very last thing I want is for you to start de-
ending me, especially to Jeff. He'd tell his cohorts and
hat would set the whole town talking about us as if we're
couple again. Miss Partridge is bad enough."

"The former librarian?" Drew blinked at her nod.
"What's she got to do with anything? She's retired, isn't
he?"

"That doesn't mean she can't hear and talk," Mandy
aid, knowing she sounded grouchy and not caring. "The
lay you arrived, Miss Partridge spied you at the café in
own. She arrived here for her riding lesson, full of a silly
omantic idea about us reuniting. She says she's been pray-
ng for that to happen for years." Mandy so did not want to
alk about anything to do with their past. "Forget it. Let's
get the horses saddled and ready."

"Yeah. Sure." Drew grabbed the halters of two horses
she indicated and led them out of the paddock toward the
temporary tack room. Together they readied eleven horses
for the trek. "I do know how to saddle a horse, boss," he
said sharply when she checked the cinch on each.

"Of course you do. Otherwise you wouldn't be Ben's
son." Finished, Mandy ignored his frown. "But I wouldn't

be his foreman if I didn't make sure everything was in
order for this group of kids. Would I?" she pressed.

"Fine." Drew didn't pursue it. Instead he made sure the
reins of each animal were firmly secured to the rail. Then
he followed her to where a big red bus had just pulled in.

Preteen boys poured out of it, and with them Drew felt
a return of his former reticence. His hands clenched into
fists as he asked himself why he'd said he'd do this.

Mandy's glance slid from his hands to his face. It was
clear she felt sorry for him.

"You probably won't remember names at first," she
murmured. "Except for one. That's our problem child in
the expensive riding boots. And next to him is his cohort
Addison, nicknamed Addy. He likes to play tricks, but a
firm word usually cures him of misbehavior."

"Not Bailey?" Drew asked, studying her.

"You wish." Mandy stepped forward and greeted the
boys in a cheery voice, welcoming them to the ranch. Then
she gave a short description of what they would see on
their horseback trip. "There will be three of us with you
today. I'm Mandy. The handsome cowboys are Drew—
and Oliver," she added hastily when the hand appeared at
Drew's side.

"Lift your hat and nod," Oliver prodded Drew. "In case
the boss didn't tell you, watch out for that kid called Bailey. He's a show-off."

"Oh, I told him," Mandy assured her ranch hand sotto
voce. "I've assigned Bailey to Mable."

"Good." Oliver grinned at Drew. "Mable's even slower
than Raven. Not that it matters. That kid will try to trade
horses with someone. Don't let him."

Advice given, Oliver conferred with Mandy to match
up horses with riders. Drew went to fetch Raven.

"Asa is riding Raven," Mandy called. Drew blinked at

her in surprise, then nodded and handed off the horse to the youngest boy, who seemed terrified.

"Do I gotta get on?" Asa asked Drew in a whimper.

Mandy watched carefully. She needed to see how Drew handled this insecure rider. That would be an important indicator of whether he really meant what he'd written in his apology letter.

"You have to get on Raven if you want to ride, Asa." Drew sounded sympathetic. When Asa visibly gulped, he asked, "You ridden much?"

"A little. But the horse was smaller." Asa cleared his throat.

"It's not hard to ride Raven. She doesn't buck or…"

You're terrifying the kid, Calhoun. Mandy stiffened, but Drew must have realized his mistake because he quickly changed tactics.

"Raven's really gentle and she loves to carry kids. You'll be very safe, Asa. You get on and I'll show you what she likes best. Foot here," he directed.

Asa couldn't quite reach the stirrup so Drew gave him a boost. Once he was seated correctly, Drew went through the basics. Relieved, Mandy saw the boy gradually relax.

"Drew's a good teacher, Asa," Mandy called encouragingly. "He's been riding horses for a long time and he knows everything. You need any help, you ask him, okay?"

"Uh-huh." The boy smiled shyly, peeking at Drew from beneath his too-large hat.

Though Drew forced a smile, Mandy knew he was suddenly aware that the entire group was watching him. She also knew he didn't like all the attention.

"Okay?" she asked.

"Yeah. Upset stomach," he mumbled. "Maybe I shouldn't have had that second helping at lunch."

It wasn't the food and they both knew it. But Mandy wasn't going to press him.

"You'll be okay," she soothed.

"Sure."

Mandy's heart sank at his glare. Drew had opened his heart to her once, long ago, when they were more than friends. But they weren't friends now. They would make this work only if both of them avoided asking too many questions.

"What am I riding today, Mandy?" Drew inquired.

"Golden Girl. Jo Jo's Dream came up lame this morning and Arabella's off her feed so I had to switch. It's good because Bonnie's horse needs the exercise." She mentally hit the off switch on the past one more time. *Drew's just here for a few weeks to help. Nothing more.*

"Great." Drew walked over to a big bay Bonnie had named Golden Girl when she was a foal. He swung himself into the saddle, waiting as Mandy gave the group directions.

"Sorry. Habit. I forgot that's your job now," she muttered a few minutes later with a grimace as Oliver lined up the kids in pairs.

"No problem," he said in a dull voice that didn't sound like the Drew she used to know. When horses and riders were ready, he nudged his horse toward the path. Mandy blocked it.

"We go this way, Drew. It's new." She spoke softly so the kids wouldn't overhear. "Ben thinks it's harder for them to get off this trail."

He didn't look pleased that she'd omitted to warn him. Mandy shrugged it off.

"I forgot to tell you that yesterday. Sorry." She sighed when he didn't respond. "You lead. Oliver will stay in the middle. I'll take the back end," she murmured.

Drew nodded without arguing and moved to lead the

way. Judging by his posture, he was ill at ease for about two seconds. Then it was as if time stood still, like old times.

Mandy had always loved trail rides. The wind playing with newly budded leaves, the smell of horses and chatter from the kids drew her back to the moment. Asa was asking her a question. Sensing Drew was listening, Mandy concentrated on the nervous boy.

"You're doing very well, Asa. If I had a little boy—" She choked off her words and her face lost all color. She had to stop letting the past revive its head. She had to deal with the here and now. "Don't hang on to the reins so tightly, okay? Raven knows she has to follow the other horses—whoa!"

She pulled on Asa's reins and her own simultaneously, suddenly aware that the entire line had stopped. She glanced up, amazed to see Drew cantering along the path's edge until he was beside them.

Mandy sighed. Why couldn't he just do what she'd asked?

Lord, give me strength.

Mandy was doing *his* job.

That had to change if he was truly in charge here.

Drew nodded at Oliver as he rode past. When he reached the end of the line, he spoke quietly but firmly.

"I'd like you to take the lead, Mandy, please."

"What's wrong?" she asked in surprise.

"Nothing. But I can't see what's happening with my back to everyone. There are some great things to notice on this part of the ranch." He ignored the voice in his head that scoffed at the idea that he really wanted to chat with a bunch of kids. "That's what I'm here for, isn't it?"

"Yes, it is," she agreed with a grin. "You're sure?" At

his nod, she wheeled her horse out of the line and rode to the front. Asa watched her leave with a glum look.

"Everything okay, Asa?" Drew asked. "You're not too uncomfortable?"

"I'm okay. I guess." Asa pressed his heels against the horse's flanks and fell into last place in the now moving line.

"You don't like it out here?" Drew rode alongside him, determined to do this right. Ben had long ago taught that the best guides made sure their guests got the most out of every adventure. Maybe the only thing Asa would get out of this ride was to see the ranch with new eyes. Drew tried to view it from Asa's perspective.

"It's pretty, but—it's so big." The words seemed to burst out of the boy as he gazed around him.

"Yes, it is," Drew agreed. "There's nothing to be afraid of."

"Bailey told me there's bears here." Asa glanced fearfully over his shoulder as if an attack was imminent.

"Sometimes bears do come on this part of the ranch," Drew agreed. "But it's usually in the fall when they have cubs and want to feed on the berries. If you look way over there, where you see those black-and-white cows, that's where the berries grow, and they're nowhere near ready to eat yet. So no worries. Anyway, bears don't bother people riding horses."

"Oh." Asa rode on, but his frown remained.

"Things aren't always what they seem. For instance, see those green plants with the white, kind of tufted tops?" Drew pointed, waited for the boy's nod. "That's bear grass, but that doesn't mean bears eat it. Sometimes they use it to make beds on. Bear grass only blooms once every seven years so it's special you get to see it today." Drew kind of liked the way Asa's eyes widened at the information. "Those purple flowers with the yellow centers are called alpine daisies. And over there you can see a whitetail deer and her fawn."

Drew kept pointing out things, his voice low because he hoped the animals would stick around long enough for the other kids to notice.

"Those are sheep on those rocks, right?" Asa looked more relaxed now.

"You're right." Though Drew still didn't care for having the responsibility of kids, at least this one was trying to learn. "Above them are mountain goats. They are very nimble and can really jump."

"They can stick you with their horns and kill you," a voice chirped.

Drew stifled his irritation as Asa gripped his reins so tightly his fingertips began turning white.

There could be no doubt as to which child had said that.

"Newbies often think that about mountain goats, Bailey, but it's wrong," Drew corrected in a firm tone. "The goats are wild and they like it that way. They won't come anywhere near you, Asa."

Because Bailey had left his place and others followed, the line had stopped. Mandy and Oliver were struggling to get them back in order, but to Drew it looked as effective as herding sheep. He stuck his fingers between his teeth and whistled. The shrill noise startled everyone, including the wildlife, which scattered. The kids stared at him in surprise. So did Mandy. Oliver grinned.

"Hey, guys. Remember we said you must stay in a line? That's a rule we all have to follow." Drew waited. Sheepishly, with Oliver and Mandy's help to turn some stubborn horses, the boys moved into more orderly positions.

Except Bailey.

"Why do we have to stay in a line?" he demanded.

"Because that's how we ride the trail and because I say so." Drew saw Mandy turn. He figured she was about to take charge, so he spoke quickly. "This is the path that we prepared for you to ride on, Bailey. It's safe and familiar to the horses. But if you go off it, your horse could step in a hole or stumble. Or you could be hurt."

"My dad said—"

"Your dad isn't here, Bailey. I am, and because I'm in charge of you and this trail ride, I need you to obey. Now. Or you could go back to the ranch and wait for us to return." Drew held the kid's glare with a steady stare until the boy resumed his place. Sort of. "Since we're stopped now…"

Drew paused. The group's attention focused on him. He didn't like the spotlight, and yet… Maybe Bonnie and Ben had never been able to make the ranch his home, but they'd certainly taught Drew about where he lived. He needed to share that, even though the thought of it choked him up.

God? Help? He felt guilty for asking when he hadn't prayed in years.

"I want to tell you about this area of our ranch where a wildfire went through some years ago."

Deliberately keeping his eyes off Mandy so he could concentrate on the kids, Drew took a deep breath, marshaled his thoughts and slowly repeated Ben's explanation of how fire was a rancher's enemy because of the heavy cost it could exact. The kids seemed interested so Drew then related that there were also benefits to fire, from helping start new spruce tree growth to getting rid of pests that could ruin the forest.

"So that's how things work together on a ranch," he finished, shocked that he'd managed to get his spiel out without the usual difficulties.

"'Cause, just like Ben always says at Sunday school, God makes all things work together, right, Drew?" Asa grinned at him.

"Yeah. Right." Drew cleared his throat, too aware of

every eye on him, especially Mandy's. He should have remembered that most of these kids attended Bonnie and Ben's church. "Any questions?" After answering a couple of simple queries about the horses, he saw genuine interest on Bailey's face. Maybe he could pursue that. "Okay, guys, let's move on. Don't want to be late for dinner."

He risked a quick glance at Mandy, stupidly relieved when she gave him an approving thumbs-up. Oliver winked at him, too, before moving his horse behind Bailey's as if he didn't quite trust the kid. Somewhat heartened that his prayer for help had been answered, Drew nudged his horse onward.

As the kids chatted back and forth, Drew kept a sharp eye out for problems. Things happened to kids that couldn't be fixed, and then they were left to deal with them for the rest of their lives. He'd lived that so he wasn't about to be the cause of someone else's lifelong issues.

They stopped twice more before reaching the chuck wagon, which was loaded with food for starving boys. As the kids rushed to dismount, Drew reminded them to first water their horses at the trickling stream before tying the reins to an old-fashioned hitching post that someone, probably Ben, had installed.

"You did really well, Drew." Mandy matched his steps as they led their horses to water.

"Thanks." Why did that simple sentence from her make him feel so good?

"The kids had a great time looking for all the things you spoke about, and that story of you learning to ride when you first came to Hanging Hearts Ranch was really helpful for our two newest riders." She studied the smiling faces of the boys who were perched on fallen logs or tree stumps, balancing their food on their knees as they carried on animated discussions. "You even had Bailey enthralled. You're going to be really good at this."

"I should be. I've done enough riding with Ben, heard his stories a hundred times. I must have absorbed something." He waited while the horses drank, uneasy next to her, yet not eager to get away either. "I'm sorry you felt you had to come along. I'm sure it's a waste of time you'd rather have spent with Ella."

"I do love spending time with her," she agreed as a smile tipped up the corners of her lips. "But I have to do my job, too. She understands."

"But—" Drew stopped short and rethought the critical comment he'd been about to utter. This truce between them had to last, for his parents' sakes.

"You're thinking she's only five and she shouldn't have to understand." Mandy nodded, sober-faced. "I agree. But every kid has to face hard facts in their lives. Ella and I are more blessed than most to be living here on this lovely ranch. Besides, she loves her caregiver."

Mandy moved away to loop her reins over the hitching post. She walked to the food wagon and chose a few things for her plate. Drink in hand, she found a patch of grass to sit on and began eating.

Drew selected his own food and then, despite a wealth of misgiving, he sat down next to her.

"Have you completely given up on the idea of vet school?" he asked, mostly to break the silence with which Mandy seemed totally comfortable.

"For now. Maybe forever." She chewed a stalk of celery thoughtfully. "I don't know. Ella comes first. Work second."

"So—it depends?" Drew chuckled at her surprised look. "You always used to say that. Some things never change."

"I say it because nothing in life is a sure thing. It always depends." She bit into her corn cob with relish.

"I wouldn't have thought you'd hold that view, given your strong faith." Drew wished he hadn't said it because now the air between them crackled with tension. "I'm sorry. That just kind of slipped out."

"I know you don't trust God, Drew. I know you don't think I should either. You never did," she said very quietly. "You've always had this chip on your shoulder, daring God to prove Himself to you. The thing is, He doesn't have to. He's God and—"

An argument burst out. Of course Bailey was involved.

"Go," Mandy urged when Drew glanced at her. "But be warned. Sooner or later you and I are going to finish this discussion."

As he separated the two kids, Drew dearly hoped it would happen later. Actually never. He did not want to rehash his issues about God with Mandy again.

What he wanted was to leave, as fast as he could, before he got any more involved.

Not gonna happen, cowboy, his brain jeered.

That evening Mandy sat next to Ella, stargazing on their favorite hillside perch just below the spot where they'd buried Blackie. Ella loved waiting for shooting stars, and since the evenings were now warmer, Mandy intended to make sure it happened more often once school was over.

"Look, Mama. A big one." Ella pointed, holding her breath until the light faded into nothing. "God sure is smart to make so many stars," she whispered, leaning her head against Mandy's shoulder.

"He sure is. Shooting stars are just one of the special gifts He made for us. Because He loves us." Mandy lifted her little girl into her lap. "'For God so loved the world,'" she quoted, then paused to let Ella continue.

"'He gave His onliest son…'" Ella turned to look at Mandy, her face scrunched up in her thinking style. "Did Jesus have a mom?"

"Mary. Remember the Christmas story?"

"Yeah, but I mean a mom in heaven, where He lived with His dad before He was a baby in a manger?" When her mother didn't immediately answer, Ella jumped to her feet. "Hey, there's Drew. I'm gonna ask him."

"No, Ella—" *Save your breath, Mandy.* She remained in place, watching her daughter race up to Drew and grab at his pant leg while she asked her question.

Drew stared at Ella and then searched the dusky yard until his gaze finally found Mandy. He walked toward her with Ella trying to keep up.

"Stop, Drew!" the little girl finally shouted in exasperation.

"What?" He blinked and then studied her with a confused look. "Your mother is over there."

"I know. We're watching the stars. But you're going too fast." As if to prevent him from leaving her behind again, Ella slid her tiny hand into his larger one. "Mama doesn't know if Jesus had a mommy when He lived with God in heaven, so I asked you."

"Yeah, but, uh—" Drew blinked in bewilderment. "I don't know."

Mandy almost laughed out loud. She was used to Ella's sudden and unusual questions. Clearly Drew was not.

"Well, if you don't know and Mama don't know, them who'm I s'posed to ask?" Ella demanded.

"Sometimes mommies and da—" Aghast, Mandy stopped herself just in time. "Sometimes adults don't have all the answers to kids' questions," she rephrased. She couldn't tell if Drew realized how close she'd come to blurting out the truth.

"You were gonna say daddies," Ella said, brows drawn together. "But I don't got a daddy." She made a mad face. "So who knows about Jesus's mom?" She crossed her little arms across her chest and waited.

Mandy glanced at Drew, who lifted his shoulders in a

response she translated to mean *don't look at me. I haven't got a clue.*

"Well, honey, that's probably a good question for Pastor Joe," Mandy suggested.

"Or maybe your Sunday school teacher," Drew mumbled.

"She doesn't like it when I ask questions. She says I ask too many." Ella tipped her head to one side to study Drew. "Wanna watch stars fall with us?"

"Maybe for a few minutes." He sat on the grass and leaned back on his elbows. "Are there lots tonight?"

"Yep." Ella planted herself on the grass right next to him and copied his actions. "Mama said you took some boys riding. Did you like it?"

"I guess. I went on that trail a long time ago with Ben. It was nice to go again." Drew glanced at Mandy. "Your mom helped."

"She always does." Ella shrugged as if she found that perfectly normal. "Auntie Bonnie says God put us on this earth to be helpers for each other, an' she says Mama is the bestest helper there ever was." She turned to study Drew, her face perplexed. "She is a really good mama," she said softly. "Only…"

"Only what?" Mandy asked, anxious about her daughter's confused tone.

Drew also seemed to realize that Ella was troubled about something because he sat up and studied her. "Hey, what's wrong, Ella?"

"I want a daddy." Her daughter burst into tears, big sobs heaving her little chest as she turned against Drew and wept her heart out. "I prayed an' I prayed, but God didn't get me a daddy and Mama says she can't get me one neither."

"Oh." Drew tentatively brushed her head but his gaze rested on Mandy. "I'm sorry, Ella."

"Mama's sorry, too," Ella said sadly. "But that don't help. I need a daddy."

"Why?" Drew asked.

"To love me." Ella glared at him, her frustration evident. "Don'tcha know what a dad is s'posed to do, Drew? He's s'posed to love his kids and take care of them an' make sure nothing bad happens to them. An' if it does, he's gotta fix it. I don't got a daddy to fix things for me."

"Ella, sweetie, we don't have anything that needs fixing," Mandy murmured, trying to reassure her. "We're fine."

Ella jumped up, her face awash in tears, and scowled at both of them.

"No, we aren't!" she shouted. "We aren't fine at all!" Then she whirled around and raced into the house.

"Aren't you going after her?" Drew demanded when Mandy didn't immediately follow.

"I will, but Ella needs a moment. She doesn't like it if I go to her too quickly. After an outburst, she always says she needs to talk to God first," she explained.

Drew didn't say anything for a minute, but it was clear Ella's explosion bothered him.

"There must be something wrong at school," he said finally.

Mandy shook her head. "Ella loves school and the friends she has there. It isn't that."

"Then what?" Drew stared at her as if she was deliberately withholding the answer he wanted.

"I don't know. That's what we have to find out," Mandy said tiredly as she got up.

"We?" Drew frowned.

"I meant me. *I* have to figure it out. And I will. Good night." She walked away, forcing herself to maintain an even stride, as if she had all the confidence in the world that she could sort out this issue of Ella's, as she had all her previous ones.

But inside Mandy was scared.

Drew will never be the kind of father Ella described, God.

So now what?

Chapter Five

Sunday mornings were Mandy's favorite time.

Just her and her daughter. Together.

"That was a yummy breakfast, Mama." Ella's sunny smile grew as she licked the sticky maple syrup off her fingertips, her face glowing with happiness. "We never made pancakes with chocolate chips and peaches before."

"I know. Good, huh?" Mandy shoved the pile of chocolate off the edge of her plate into the garbage. She loved the treat as much as the next woman, but not at eight in the morning and definitely not with pancakes. "I'm thinking next week we should try onions," she teased.

"Yuck." Ella peered out the window. "There's Drew. We should 'vite him to breakfast. He hasn't got nobody to eat with."

"Anybody," Mandy corrected automatically. "You'd better go wash up so we can get ready for church."

"I gotta talk to Drew first." Ella was out the door before Mandy could stop her. Sighing heavily, she followed, hoping against hope that the daddy issue wouldn't come up again. "Good morning," she greeted Drew, shocked by his haggard appearance.

"Morning." His voice sounded rumbly and hoarse.

"Are you sick, Drew?" Ella asked as she slid her hand into his.

"No. I was working all night." He must have noticed Mandy's surprise. "It's the best time to see what the overseas markets are doing on Monday. I had a report to make."

"The trail rides interfere with your work, don't they? I'm sorry." Dismayed to realize that she'd set her own agenda without thinking about Drew's work, Mandy made a mental note to ensure he had a copy of the booking sheet. Maybe then he could avoid future all-nighters.

Although a part of her acknowledged that his stubbly look was definitely attractive.

"The ride didn't interfere. That's when I always work. Your hands are really sticky, Ella." Drew eased his hand from hers and grimaced as he flexed his fingers. "Have you been eating candy already this morning?"

"Nope. Pancakes. Mama makes the best." She tilted her head to study him. "What did you eat for breakfast?"

"Nothing. I don't eat breakfast. Just coffee," Drew responded.

"That's bad. Teacher said so." Ella's disapproval radiated across her face. "You're supposed to eat nu—nut—" She thought for a moment. "Food that's good for you. So you can do things and be strong."

"What did you have for breakfast that made your hands sticky?" Drew asked.

Uh-oh. Mandy wanted to interrupt but Ella was too quick.

"Pancakes with chocolate chips and peaches. It was delish." Ella's grin was infectious because even Drew was smiling faintly.

"And sausages," Mandy added.

"Ah, the nutrition part." Drew chuckled at her glower. "You're not quite as strict a mother as I expected."

Mandy wasn't sure what that meant. She would have asked but—

"We got some pancake stuff left. You can have it, if you want," Ella offered.

"Thanks. I'd like that," Drew said.

Mandy blinked in surprise. He *wanted* to eat with them?

"Come on." Ella took his hand again, giggling when he tried to avoid her touch. "You'll be sticky, too," she promised.

Not quite sure why Drew was agreeing to this, Mandy followed them into her home, wishing, when he glanced around, that she'd straightened up.

"This looks cozy," he said.

"That's a good word for it." She pointed. "We eat over there." She waited for Drew to sit before arranging a plate and cutlery in front of him. "I'll have the pancakes ready in a second."

"Oh, I thought Ella meant they were already cooked." He frowned. "I didn't mean to give you more work, Mandy."

"It's not much work to cook a few pancakes. The batter is made." She set the skillet on the stove and waited for it to heat. "Do you want both chocolate chips and peaches?"

"Uh, maybe just a bit of peach on one," he said hesitantly.

"You gotta try the chocolate, Drew," Ella protested. "Mama, make him try a little bit. That's what you always say to me."

"Yes, I do, because experiencing things is important." Mandy arched her brows at Drew.

"Fine. I'll try it," he agreed glumly, probably to escape Ella's expectant face.

Hiding her smile, Mandy poured batter onto the skillet and dropped in a few chips. She took her time arranging the peach slices into a happy face, though why she was taking such care for Drew wasn't immediately clear in her mind.

But then, as she flipped the pancakes, Mandy decided she was doing this for Ella, because she wanted Drew to share something with their daughter, even if it was only the love of Ella's favorite meal.

"Here you are," she said, setting the plate in front of Drew. "This coffee's almost fresh."

"Thank you." He grabbed the mug and almost inhaled the dark brew before sighing. "I'm lousy at making coffee. Can't you teach me?"

Surprised he'd think she could teach him anything, Mandy said, "It's simple."

"Not for me." He took another swig before shaking his head. "I can cook pretty much anything. But I cannot make coffee."

"You cook?" She gaped at him.

"Yes. Because I like to eat." He shrugged. "What's so weird about that?"

"I just never—"

"Taste the pancakes, Drew," Ella ordered. Mandy cleared her throat. "Please," the little girl quickly added.

"Here goes." Drew poked through, probably to find a piece with the fewest chocolate chips. As if summoning his courage, he took a breath before sliding the fork into his mouth. His dark eyes widened in surprise as he chewed. "Hey, this is really good."

Mandy rolled her eyes. Drew had always had a sweet tooth. She got busy cooking more pancakes. Ella disappeared to get ready for church, which left an awkward gap of silence. Mandy ran water into the sink and generally made a lot of noise, hoping that would make it difficult to hold a conversation. A few minutes later, having run out of excuses, she saw surprise flood Drew's face and turned to see her daughter wearing her fanciest dress, a velvet one she'd worn to be flower girl at a friend's wedding.

"Wow! You look very nice, Ella." Drew leaned back in his chair.

"Honey, it's supposed to be warm today. That dress—" Mandy watched the determined glitter grow in her daughter's dark eyes and gave up. "Don't complain to me if you're too hot in church," she warned.

"I won't. Are you wearing that to church?" Ella asked Drew in disapproval.

"I wasn't actually planning—"

"You c'n wear jeans, but nicer ones. Those are ripped." Ella crossed her arms over her chest. "So's your shirt. An' your hair's all mussy. Miss Partridge doesn't like mussy hair. She'll talk to you 'bout it," she warned.

Drew looked so trapped by just the thought of conversation with Miss Partridge that Mandy wanted to hoot with laughter. Shouldn't a grown man be over his childhood fear of the town's former librarian? But she kept a serious face and her lips locked. Let Drew get out of this on his own.

"I wasn't going to go to church this morning, Ella," he explained as he finished his coffee and pushed away his plate. "But I guess I should, if only to thank folks for helping out Ma and Pops."

"That would be nice," Mandy agreed, keeping her back turned. "I know everyone in town would like to see you again. Especially Miss Partridge."

"You sure know how to spread cheer," Drew said dryly as he rose. "Thank you for the breakfast and the coffee. It was as good as Ella promised."

Mandy's heart pinched when he smiled at their daughter. Ella almost glowed with happiness at his attention. What would happen to her precious child when Drew left?

"Oh, may I catch a ride with you?" he asked, stopping in the doorway.

"Bonnie's car is here. I'm sure she won't mind if you use it while you're here." Fear of spending intimate moments in the car with Drew had her blurting out the words before she could stop them. Immediately Mandy regretted saying that because it made her look defensive. "I should have told you that before. The problem is, it has a flat. Since we're both going to church, you're more than welcome to join us for the ride. Can you be ready in half an hour?"

"Why so early?" he asked, frowning.

"There's a baby dedication for my friends, the Hanovers, this morning and it will be crowded. There's usually a huge turnout to witness parents promising to raise their child for God," she added, interpreting his frown as an objection. "But we have Sunday school classes first."

"Ah." He nodded. "Half an hour." Then he was gone, loping across the yard to his parents' home.

Mandy heaved a sigh of relief, trying to release the spring of tension that had overtaken her body. She always found baby dedications difficult, often fighting tears as the parents promised to raise their child as God directed. The solemn words always reminded her of when she'd been pregnant and she'd promised... No!

Mandy inhaled, drawing on her inner strength. She hoped Drew wouldn't sit with them. If she got teary-eyed during the dedication, he'd ask questions. But that concern wasn't enough to cause her to miss her friends' special event.

There was also the matter of the local gossips and how they'd interpret Drew's presence on the ranch as more than just a helping hand. In the year and a half since Mandy had returned, it had taken a steady focus on work for gossip about her and Ella to die down.

Now that Drew was back, would it begin all over again? She couldn't let that happen. Her punishment for disobeying one of God's rules about love and marriage was to remain alone. She'd promised that when Ella was born. Drew's reappearance couldn't change anything.

Mandy whispered a prayer for courage as she did the dishes, knowing it was going to take every bit of resolve and control she possessed to walk into the church beside Drew and face people who'd known them back when.

But what other choice did she have?

"Wear your prettiest dress today, Mama." Ella bounced from one foot to the other. "The blue one."

Mandy trailed her daughter into the bedroom. Drawing attention to herself wasn't smart, but some internal longing made her want to show Drew she was more than just a plain rancher.

"Why that one?" she asked.

"'Cause you look so pretty in it. God wants us to look pretty, doesn't He?"

"I guess He does, honey." Mandy slid the flowery cotton sateen sundress over her head and let it glide down her body. She fastened plain silver earrings and braided her hair, adding a dark blue clip. A touch of eyeshadow, mascara and lip gloss, and she was ready.

"Not those old shoes, Mama." Ella dug in the closet. "These."

Mandy gulped at the four-inch heels swinging from Ella's hand. She'd forgotten she owned them. She slid her feet in between the straps and stood. Hopefully she wouldn't fall flat on her face.

"Mama, you look so beautiful," Ella breathed in awe.

"Thank you. So do you, sweetheart." Maybe clothes really did make the woman because for the first time in a long while, Mandy felt attractive.

Exhaling, she led the way out to her car and gulped at the sight of immaculately attired Drew who stood waiting with one hip against her front fender.

Was it wrong to feel a wiggle of satisfaction when he stared at her?

Mandy didn't know. And didn't care. She simply savored it.

Mandy was more beautiful than ever. Was it the maturity in her face, those jutting cheekbones and clear emerald eyes that added to her attraction? That dress certainly helped. And those heels...

"I'll drive," he said, drawing open the passenger door.

"That's not necessary... Um, okay."

Drew stared as Mandy, whom he'd never known to be mercurial, changed her mind midsentence and handed him the keys before swinging her legs into her car.

Ella climbed into her car seat in the back and quickly fastened her belt as if she was in a hurry. She was an independent child, his—Mandy's daughter. Drew had no claim on this child. *I don't want one. Remember?*

He shoved away his thoughts and took the driver's seat.

"Bonnie said you live in New York. Do you drive a lot in the city?" Mandy's voice sounded stilted, as if she felt she had to make conversation.

"Not much. Parking's a nightmare and anyway, the subway's so easy." He surveyed the valleys and the mountains beyond and smiled. "New York is nothing like Hanging Hearts Ranch."

"Do you like the crush of people and traffic there?" she mused.

"I'm used to it. Since I work alone a lot, it's sometimes nice to lose yourself in the city's busyness. And there are lots of places I can have breakfast at two in the afternoon. Not pancakes, peaches and chocolate, but still." Drew grinned at her droll expression. "What about you? Ever have a hankering to return to the lights of Missoula?"

"Goodness, no!" She half shuddered. "I was a misfit

there. Hanging Hearts Ranch is where I belong. With the animals."

"Not looking like that," he murmured appreciatively. "What about the winters? You never liked the cold." He remembered them skating on the ice rink his parents had made.

"It wasn't the cold I hated, Drew." Mandy rolled her eyes. "It was the endless hours you made me spend pushing around a puck."

"When you wanted to do double and triple axels." He laughed while privately wondering how he could coax a little more speed from her vehicle. "I haven't forgotten that."

"Mama teached me to skate," Ella piped up from the back. "But I can't do jumps and spins like she does."

"Your mother is the queen of spins, Bella Ella." Drew didn't want to recall the past, but memories of moments he'd spent with Mandy riding, hiking, skating and swimming flooded his brain like crystal drops. Happy precious moments that had made his youth fun just because she was there. How had they lost that?

"What's Bella mean?" Ella demanded and grinned when Drew said beautiful.

"Lately I feel like I'm spinning a lot." Mandy peeked at him through her lashes. "How about you? Is your schedule here too much?'

"It was rough at first," he admitted. "But it's getting easier. Oliver is amazing. He always seems to know exactly who to keep an eye on."

"He's been a real blessing since he arrived."

Mandy didn't say any more and Drew wondered why, especially since Oliver had never offered any details of his past life.

"Oh, boy." Mandy grimaced as they drove into the church parking lot. "There's already a ton of people here.

I'd hoped—" She cut off whatever she'd been going to say, leaving Drew wondering.

He pulled into an empty space and slid the gearshift into Park.

"Problem?" Mandy's smirk confused him.

"Old people park here. What are the grandmas and grandpas called again, Mama?" Ella's seat belt clinked as she unclasped it and wiggled forward. "I c'n never 'member that word."

"Seniors." Mandy waited patiently while her daughter repeated it.

Miss Partridge stood by the church, eyeing them with one arched eyebrow. Drew wanted to get inside before she could accost them and lecture him as she had so often in the past, until Ella's comment penetrated.

"I'm in the seniors' parking area? I didn't see a sign." Drew grimaced, certain Miss Partridge would point out his faux pas the minute they went inside. "Put your belt on again, Ella. I'll find a new spot."

"'Cause we're not seniors, right, Drew?" Her seat belt clicked.

"Not yet, Bella." Drew headed for the farthest corner of the lot, his satisfaction multiplying when Miss Partridge paused midstep to watch them move away. After a moment she readjusted her feathered hat, shook her head and marched inside the church. He knew she'd be lying in wait for him.

"Uh, Drew?" Mandy touched his arm. "This isn't church property."

Clenching his jaw, he knew he'd gone too far because his focus hadn't been on driving. He backed up, parked and got out.

"Don't you dare say a word," he ordered as he held Mandy's door open.

She managed to stay silent, probably because she was

concentrating on not letting her spiky heels sink into the gravel. Drew relented and held out his arm, which Mandy grabbed with thanks. Ella clasped his other hand, chattering a mile a minute as they walked to the church. Drew had no clue what she said. He was trying to mentally prepare himself for going back to the place where his questions about God had never been answered.

They'd barely entered the foyer when Miss Partridge appeared.

"Don't look so mad," Mandy breathed. "Smile and pretend you really want to be here. Good morning, Miss Partridge," she said in a bright, cheery voice. "My, what a lovely hat. I've never seen such a big feather."

"Thank you, dear." The former librarian preened and patted her sausage curls. "I designed it myself."

"You certainly have a talent." Mandy listened to her explain hat-making, nodded and then excused herself to take Ella to her class. "The adults meet in the fireside room," she told Drew.

"Don't worry about him, dear. I'll make sure he gets there." Miss Partridge latched on to Drew's arm and forcefully tugged. "It's nice to see you and Mandy together again. You make such a lovely couple."

"We're not—" Drew never got a chance to finish his denial.

"Though you've been home several times, I don't believe you've attended since our renovations here were completed," Miss Partridge pointed out briskly.

"No." What else could he say?

"I helped design the renovations," she announced proudly.

"Stunning," Drew murmured, knowing that was expected. "The color combination is very, er, uplifting."

"I always think purple is so regal. This is our new fireside room." She chose a chair, then patted the one next to hers. "Sit right here, dear."

"Thank you." With no escape available, Drew sat.

"Mandy looks especially beautiful today. For you?" Miss Partridge batted her lashes coquettishly, her curious gaze searching for something, anything to tell the world.

"We are not a couple." There, he'd made that clear, not that he thought it would make much difference to this woman. "And Mandy's always been beautiful," he added.

"She doesn't often wear dresses to church." Miss Partridge leaned closer and whispered, "She does such mannish work, you know. I think she finds it difficult to be ladylike on Sundays. Why, she often even wears jeans here," she said in a slightly scandalized voice.

"I see a lot of other folks do, also. Like me," Drew pointed out, irritated by her denigration of Mandy. "I can't imagine anyone questioning Mandy's femininity no matter what she wears."

In fact, several of the men were smiling as Mandy entered the room. She greeted each person by name, friendly but nothing more.

"It's good to hear you defend her, Drew. Obviously she's someone you care about. Oh, there's Edna. I need to tell her something. Excuse me?" Miss Partridge darted away.

Drew exhaled and gave up. From the day he'd first arrived here, he'd never been able to get in the last word with Miss Partridge. Apparently nothing had changed.

"You're making our eyes pop today, girl," one of the older men said to Mandy. "Those shoes look a lot nicer than your boots."

"Thank you, Marcus." Mandy thrust out her foot and studied her shoe. She seemed to have no idea of her beauty. "You should tell Ella. She chose them."

"Kid has good taste," Marcus praised.

Drew studied the guffawing older males, but his gaze

quickly returned to Mandy. She seemed—embarrassed?—by their attention. But then she'd always preferred to be one of the group, never a show-off, except when she was trick riding or figure skating.

"Well, sorry, guys, but come next Sunday, the boots will be back. Can't work in these heels." Amid a chorus of teasing boos, she sat down next to Drew in Miss Partridge's chair. "Okay if I sit here?" she asked him belatedly.

"Perfect." Overly conscious of the curious looks directed his way, Drew knew the former librarian had been talking about him and Mandy. He didn't want people speculating about the two of them, and yet, he felt oddly proud sitting next to this woman. Why that was, he didn't want to contemplate. "What happens now?"

"We usually have a teaching time while the kids are in Sunday school," she explained. "It's a little different setup than when we were kids, but the lessons are so good. John Purdy is very knowledgeable Biblically, and even better at sharing what he knows. He moved to Sunshine a year ago."

Admiration laced her voice. That made Drew curious. "Which one is he?"

"He's not here yet. I'll introduce you later." Mandy opened her bulletin.

Drew mentally sighed at the thought of sitting through two sermons, this John fellow's and then the pastor's. Why had he accepted Ella's breakfast offer?

Because you're tired of always being alone? Because you wanted to be with Mandy and Ella? He brushed aside that inner voice.

"We usually grab a coffee," Mandy told him. "Want one?"

"Always." Drew followed her to a bar where coffee supplies were laid out. Expecting some generic dishwater blend, Drew was pleasantly surprised when he resumed his seat and took a sip.

"Good, isn't it?" Mandy grinned. "John insists he can't teach if there isn't good coffee to be had. He orders a special blend just for this class."

"If he can make coffee in a big urn like that taste this good, I need to meet John." Drew cradled his cup and leaned back as a tall, wiry cowboy strode to a lectern and opened his Bible.

Miss Partridge scurried into a seat across the room. She showed no sign of dismay at losing her spot. In fact, the lady winked at him.

Hoping the coffee would keep him alert, Drew soon realized he needn't have worried about nodding off. John's teaching on the book of Revelation kept him so focused, he started at the sound of a buzzer ending the session. John dismissed the group, then walked toward them.

"Hey, Mandy."

"John, I don't think you've met Bonnie and Ben's son, Drew." Mandy's huge smile made Drew wonder if she had a soft spot for the rancher who did not, he noticed, wear a wedding ring.

"Pleased to meet you, Drew." A flicker of curiosity lit the teacher's blue eyes.

"Drew's home to lend a hand while his parents recuperate," Mandy explained.

"Oh, so you're a rancher, too." The other man nodded.

"No, I'm a financial analyst," Drew corrected. "Mandy's the rancher. I'm just here to do whatever she tells me." Stupidly, he felt smug satisfaction at John's blink of surprise.

"Oh. Well, welcome to our class. It's an interesting study. Excuse me. I need to speak to a board member about supplies."

"You're just here to do whatever I tell you?" Mandy arched one eyebrow, her tone acerbic. "Since when?"

"Is John someone special to you?" How Drew wished

he could withdraw that stupid question. It was none of his business. But Mandy had always been his girl.

She dumped you, dummy.

"All my friends are special." Mandy tucked her bag under her arm, then lifted her head to study him. "But not in the way you mean."

"Why not? He's okay in the looks department."

"John is exceptional in the looks department," she corrected with a tiny smile that sent a new spark of irritation to Drew's brain. "He is, however, coming out of a bad relationship. Besides which, neither of us are interested. And before you ask, I have more than enough on my plate with Ella and the Double H. I don't have time to figure out romance."

"Huh." He followed her to a pew in the sanctuary which, thankfully, was far away from Miss Partridge. "Doesn't Ella join us?"

"They have kids' church," she whispered as the prelude began. "It's a good way for children to learn how to sit through a service because it follows the same pattern as here, only it's at their level."

"Oh." Drew rose with everyone else as a music team led them in the first hymn, one he'd sung as a teen.

After the baby dedication, during which Mandy sniffed, blew her nose and refused to look at him, the morning followed a familiar church pattern. Announcements, lots of singing and a solo by the cowboy who'd led their adult class all led up to a sermon about new beginnings and the choice of starting over with God leading the way or falling back into the same old patterns.

Pastor Joe's comments forced Drew to ponder his return to the Double H. So far he had been following his old patterns. Maybe it was time to change that up?

Mandy's nudge to his ribs ended his musings. Drew rose hastily for the benediction, vowing to mull it over again later. As they exited the sanctuary, former friends and acquaintances stopped to greet him and offer best wishes for his parents' recovery. Mandy seemed impatient to leave—because she wanted to collect Ella? Drew made his excuses and then walked with her to find Ella. A cacophony of chattering told him kids' church was over.

"Mama." Ella raced over and grabbed her mother's skirt. "It's potluck day. Are we staying? Did we bring something to share?"

Drew couldn't translate Mandy's expression.

"I didn't bring anything, sweetie, because we're not staying," she murmured after a sideways look at Drew.

"Why not?" Ella glowered, clearly disappointed.

"Because we're going to see Auntie Bonnie and Uncle Ben, remember?" Mandy didn't look at him. "We can eat along the way."

"You're going—why didn't you tell me? I'd like to see them again." Drew tried to smother a burst of annoyance that she hadn't included him.

"I didn't plan it this way intentionally," Mandy explained softly. "But since you're escorting that ladies riding group this afternoon, I thought I'd keep quiet about our trip so you wouldn't feel bad."

Why did he always think the worst of her?

"I forgot about that group." Shocked by how much he wanted to accompany Mandy and Ella, Drew figured he'd better have a talk with himself while she and Ella were gone. "Maybe when I get some free time, I could take Bonnie's car and visit them?"

"Sure, once the flat is fixed. Oh, excuse me." She answered her phone, frowning as she listened. "Well, thank you for calling," she said. "I am so sorry about your friend. We'll try to rebook your group, but I'm not sure what openings we have left. May I call you back? By tomorrow morning for sure."

"Problem?" Drew noticed her shoulders tense. "Mandy?" he prodded when she didn't respond.

"Seems things have changed. I guess you're free to come with us to see your parents after all. The ladies riding group needs to reschedule. One of them is ill and the others don't want to go without her. That is, if you want to come along?" she added.

"I would. Thank you," he said firmly.

"So c'n we stay for potluck and c'n Drew drive Auntie Bonnie's car?" Ella begged.

"The tire—"

"I'll ask Oliver if he can change it while we eat," Drew interrupted Mandy. "He's on duty today and he was complaining about being bored. Then we can take Bonnie's, if you want."

"It's not me who wants that." Mandy didn't look thrilled.

"I do. 'Cause then we won't have to go so slow in Mama's car." Ella squealed with delight at her mother's resigned nod before racing off to tell her friends.

"So slow?" Drew couldn't figure it out.

"My car has an issue. I've had it into the garage," she said, holding up a hand to forestall his comments. "Twice. They can't find what's wrong with it. All I know is that I can't get it to go much over forty miles an hour. You must have noticed that on the way here when you kept pressing the gas pedal and nothing happened."

"So why don't you use Bonnie's car?"

"Because, as you just said, it's *Bonnie's* car. Not mine," she said in a stern voice.

"Stubborn pride," Drew muttered. "I'll drive."

"You don't have—"

"I told you I don't get to drive in the city much," he interrupted. "I'd like to do some driving while I'm here."

"Oh." Mandy studied him for several moments until she finally managed an embarrassed smile and a laugh.

"Sorry. Just trying to wrap my mind around you on the subway, surrounded by people."

"There are a lot of things you don't know about me, Mandy." Drew had no intention of explaining or discussing his city life. Nor was he going to admit it couldn't compare to the vibrant life of the ranch, or that he didn't understand why that was. "Potluck?" he prompted.

"I didn't bring anything. I never do because we usually don't stay." There was a desperate tone to her voice that he didn't comprehend until she mumbled, "I don't cook very well."

"You do excellent pancakes. Should have brought some of those," he teased, astonished that he was enjoying this repartee. "I should have kept your keys."

"Why?" She dug in her purse before tentatively extending them.

"I'll make an ice cream run. Should be back just in time for the kids' dessert. I'll be the hit of the party." Keys in hand, Drew left, threading his way through the crowd, smiling as he savored her startled look.

Mandy wasn't the only one who could manage situations.

Drew was not going to delve into why that seemed so important for him to prove to her.

Chapter Six

It was nice to be driven, to have someone else be in charge for a change, though Mandy didn't admit that aloud. Instead she concentrated on the spectacular mountain scenery.

"I like going fast," Ella chirped from the back seat. "Auntie Bonnie's car is way better."

Don't feel hurt, Mandy told herself. *Ella's a kid. Of course she appreciates bigger, faster, prettier cars. So do you.*

"Our car will be just fine for us, Ella." Once it was fixed.

"Do Ma and Pops know we're coming?" Drew seldom called the couple Mom and Dad. He'd told her once that those terms were reserved for the birth parents he'd lost. That was just one of the barriers he'd erected and never taken down since the accident, like never calling Hanging Hearts Ranch home.

"I told Bonnie we were coming last night. She won't know you've joined us though." Mandy fiddled with her purse, suddenly uncomfortable trying to make conversation with this stranger who'd been her best friend since they were nine.

"Do you call her often?" Drew asked.

"Every day, if I can. I think it must be difficult for them

to be away from the Double H as well as going through the pain of their treatment," she murmured under cover of Ella's humming. "Hopefully a daily phone call helps distract them."

"That's thoughtful." Drew glanced at her, then returned his gaze to the road. "Considering the demands you must have on your time, it's also very generous."

"Actually, I'm the one who benefits most." Mandy caught his quizzical frown and chuckled. "Somehow Bonnie always manages to cheer me up, instead of the other way around."

"Yeah, she's like that." Drew's words reminded her that while she'd had his parents to lean on these past few months, he'd had no one. As far as she knew, he never called simply to have a listening ear.

How sad that Drew had missed out on sharing his burdens with people who really cared about him and his life. Mandy suspected he didn't often call because he knew Bonnie would worry if she discerned unhappiness in his voice.

Even before they'd split, Drew had never shared much about his college life with Mandy. No doubt he'd figured she wouldn't understand his classes, and maybe she wouldn't have, but it would have been reassuring to hear his voice. Now she realized that his discomfort with talking might have kept him from opening up over the phone and had probably caused him lots of other problems, too.

Or maybe he had someone special in his world now, someone who helped him through it. Funny how that thought depressed her. So did visiting the hospital.

A wealth of memories boiled up whenever she entered hospitals and got a whiff of that medicinal smell. And this wasn't even the hospital where she'd been taken when…

Stop it. The past is over.

"It's quiet here today." Mandy watched him find the best parking spot in the hospital lot with ease.

Soon they were inside, walking down the gleaming hallway with Drew carrying the basket of fruit Mandy had insisted on bringing.

"Why did you want this?" he asked, his nose wrinkled with distaste. "I'm sure the hospital provides nutritionally satisfying meals. I doubt you have to supplement—" He broke off when she glowered at him.

"I seem to recall you once telling me how much you loved eating the baking Bonnie brought while you and your brothers were recuperating after the accident." She didn't bother to mask her irritability.

"Yes, but that was baking…" Drew gave up when she glared at him. "Never mind. It's a nice thought. I didn't bring anything."

She choked down her snappy comeback when Ella gleefully pushed open a door and bounded inside the room, squealing hello. When she reached out to Bonnie, Mandy quickly grasped her daughter's arm.

"Careful. Auntie Bonnie has hurts, remember," Mandy chided.

"I'm sorry." Ella's face wrinkled into a sad expression. "Did I hurted you, Auntie Bonnie?"

"You couldn't hurt me, darling. Now come and sit beside me and tell me what all is in this lovely fruit basket." Bonnie smiled and patted Ella's hand after Drew lifted the little girl onto the edge of the bed.

"Thank you, dear," Bonnie told him, raising one hand to cup his chin, eyes glowing. "It's lovely to see you again. How are you doing?"

"I'm supposed to ask you that, Ma." Drew bent and brushed her cheek with his lips, then touched his father on the shoulder. "Hey, Pops. What are you reading?"

"The book you gave me for Christmas. It's interesting,

once you get past the garbled first chapter." Ben grinned at him. "I bought some of that stock we talked about and I've been following it. It's gone up by twenty percent."

"How do you know that, Benjamin Halston?" Bonnie's severe look made her husband wince. "You're supposed to be recuperating."

"I recuperate much better when I check my phone and see my stock has gone up." Ben winked at Drew. "How are you doing with the trekkers?" That's what he called those he guided on his land.

"Pretty good, actually. Mandy has everything organized to a T. All I have to do is sit in the saddle and follow Oliver." Drew had deliberately made his role seem simple. Mandy knew that was because he didn't want his father worrying.

"Wasn't there a group scheduled to ride today?" Ben asked, glancing at his phone where he had the bookings recorded.

"Rescheduled," Mandy assured him. "One of them couldn't make it so the group wants to wait for her."

"Good." Ben leaned back against his pillow and began asking her questions about his herd.

Mandy answered, aware that Drew's focus wavered from his conversation with his mother because he was trying to listen in on her conversation, too. When Ben addressed his son, Mandy changed places with him.

"How's my garden?" Bonnie whispered. "Did Drew get into it?"

"You can stop whispering," he muttered in exasperation. "I tried to help weed but Mandy wouldn't let me."

"Good girl." Bonnie chuckled at his disgust. "You have other gifts, son. You're good with numbers."

"Pacification," he said plaintively.

"Absolutely." Bonnie giggled. "Have a plum."

Mandy had to smile at the repartee between the two. It was nice to see.

"Blackie died," Ella suddenly announced sadly. "Drew an' me an' Mama made him a nice box and put him in the ground aside Drew's dog what died."

"I'm very sorry, Ella. Blackie was a good friend, wasn't he?" Bonnie soothed as she wiped away a lone tear on the child's rosy cheek.

"Uh-huh." Ella sniffed.

"It's very kind of Drew to let you put Blackie near Rover. If you make Blackie a cross, maybe Mandy will paint it like she paints Rover's every spring," Ben suggested with a fond look at the little girl.

"But I thought Ma—" Drew's dark gaze rested on Mandy. "Thank you."

"No problem." Moments like this, when his barriers were down, were the most difficult because Mandy could almost let herself believe the old Drew was back.

But he wasn't and she couldn't forget that.

"Thank you for helping us out, son." Ben's bandaged hand touched Drew's.

"Drew's not gonna be my daddy," Ella announced in the moment of silence.

Mandy bit her lip, then twisted to meet Drew's wide-eyed stare as she frantically searched for something appropriate to say.

"No, I don't guess he is, honey," Ben said easily, with an easy smile at the little girl. "So you'll have to keep talking to God about that, right?"

"Yeah." Ella huffed out a gloomy sigh, then asked Bonnie to read a story from the book she'd brought along.

Mandy gulped and let out her own breath. She needed to have another chat with Ella about daddies. Soon.

"Now, son, tell me about this new company, Zippers," Ben murmured.

Mandy got a lump in her throat watching father and son bond as they discussed the stock market. How could Drew imagine he didn't belong at Hanging Hearts with this loving couple?

"Tell me how it's really going with the trail rides, Drew," Ben requested a bit later, under cover of Bonnie's voice as she told Ella a story about a princess and her family.

"Okay, I think." Drew shrugged. "I'm trying to follow your example. So far everyone seems happy enough. At least I don't think there have been any complaints."

When he glanced at her inquiringly, Mandy shook her head.

"I'm really sorry to take up your time like this," Ben said with a frown. "I know how busy you are, son."

"I'm always busy. I needed a break and I have to admit, it's nice to be riding the ranch in the spring." Drew grinned. "Takes a bit to get used to the openness though."

"I suppose," Ben agreed with a fond smile. "That first hint of green tingeing the valley is what I miss most. I wish I was there instead of here."

Mandy noticed him wince slightly as he shifted on the bed. She sent Drew a silent plea, hoping he'd reassure Ben that things were being taken care of.

"I wish you were there, too, Pops," Drew agreed.

Please don't talk about how you hate the ranch, she begged silently.

Worry dimmed Ben's smile. "How come?"

"Because then I could get a refresher course on some of those routes. You've changed several." Drew shook his head, his face rueful. "I almost messed up a couple of times last week. Thankfully Oliver was there to stop me going the wrong way."

Mandy's senses jerked awake. She hadn't heard about that.

"Oliver is one of the good guys. Doesn't say much."

Ben studied his bandaged hands. "But somehow he's always there when you need him. He's the one who doused Bonnie and me. Quick thinker."

"Are your hands bothering you? Want me to get a nurse?" Drew shifted as if to leave, but Ben shook his head.

"No pain. They're just itchy. That's what healing burns is like, I guess." The older man thought a moment, then said, "I want to tell you about that group that's coming next week. What have you got planned?"

As they talked, Mandy watched Bonnie and Ella, answered questions from the others and smiled at the appropriate times, but inside her head, her brain kept wondering if Drew had been telling Ben the truth or if he really hated being forced to step in for his father.

Or maybe it was that he hated working with her.

Drew found leaving Bonnie and Ben at the hospital difficult. It was bad enough to see them lying there, trying to hide their suffering, but leaving them alone had never hit him as hard as it did today.

"It gets to you, doesn't it?" Mandy's quiet voice penetrated the soft music that played on the car stereo, accompanied by Ella's soft snores from the back seat. "Having to walk away knowing there's nothing you can do to make it better?"

"I hate it," he said through gritted teeth.

"I do, too." A small smile lifted the corners of her lips, highlighting her beauty. "But they're getting great care in a place with people who know what to do and will make sure they're all right."

He didn't say anything. There wasn't anything to say.

"I heard you telling Ben your ideas for the ranch. What was his reaction?" she asked.

"Not much. I think he was in pain by then and talking was difficult." Drew wasn't going to remind her they were the same ideas he'd suggested to her last week, the same ideas she'd nixed. Repeatedly.

"They're good ideas, Drew, and I wish I could input them." She sounded sincere. "We just can't afford it right now. Time wise, staff wise or money wise."

"Doesn't matter. Just suggestions." Stupidly Drew had thought he could offer more than just guiding people on treks. Now he knew better. Mandy didn't want him interfering in her work, so he'd concentrate on doing what she asked him and focus on getting through the next few weeks without argument.

Ella had already overheard their bickering twice. Recently she'd begun to seek him out to demand what he and Mandy were arguing about. They had to stop.

"Ella's really tired," Mandy murmured. "She doesn't usually snore so loudly."

"Or else she's really full," Drew said with a grin. "I never saw a kid her age put away a hamburger so fast. I think she got extra fries because she was flirting with the old guy who runs the place."

"It was nice of you to buy our supper," she said.

"Ella isn't awkward around strangers at all. I'm surprised by how easily she blends in with the ranch guests." Drew had never been that easygoing. "She's very comfortable with herself, no matter if the guests are seniors or kids her age. And it doesn't seem to matter what the situation is."

"Why are you surprised?" Mandy frowned. "Aren't most kids comfortable with themselves? Until they start their teens anyway."

"I never was." Drew compared himself at nine to Ella now and came up short.

"Are we home yet?" Ella asked drowsily.

"Not yet, sweetheart. But we will be soon." Mandy reached back and pulled a small pink fuzzy blanket from a bag she'd brought. "Snuggle under this and go back to sleep."

"Okay." Mere seconds later Ella's soft snores resumed.

"She's comfortable in herself because of you," he mused aloud, realizing the truth of it. "Ella knows how much you love her and that you'll always protect her. That makes her confident." Even at his age, Drew yearned to feel the same security.

"I hope she is." Mandy checked over one shoulder before quietly asking, "How do you know how to answer her nonstop questions about a father?"

"I don't, actually. She talks an awful lot about daddies." He shrugged, reminded of Ella's questions at the diner when she'd wondered what he would order for his child to eat.

Ella's host of other queries kept Drew awake at night, pondering the scary situations that every father probably faced and the certainty that, if called upon, he'd fail.

"You always respond honestly. As her mother I know that's sometimes difficult to do." Mandy grimaced.

"Ella doesn't really want me as her father. It's probably more a case of my being here, staying here, has made her question her status quo." Drew shrugged. "Maybe some kids at school have asked about me. I think she wants to be reassured, so that's what I try to do."

Mandy remained silent for a moment before admitting, "I never know what to tell her when she asks why her friends have fathers and she doesn't."

Drew frowned. He'd never considered that from Ella's point of view, only from his own, trying to escape fatherhood. Now, realizing Ella must envy what other kids took for granted, he was reminded of his own childhood confusion. Did Ella blame God for not giving her a dad?

"How do you answer her?" Drew asked.

"Thanks to Bonnie, Ella has developed a very strong

faith in God. So I usually tell her to pray about things."
Mandy nodded. "And she does. But as we know, kids aren't patient."

"Neither are some adults I know." He grinned at her sniff of disgust.

As twilight fell, Drew drove on, lost in his thoughts of Ella, trying to picture her as a teenager, imagining the questions she'd have about boys and love and families. Would she get the answers she needed or would she feel a lack in her life, as he had? Would Mandy be able to satisfy that curious brain, or would she turn to someone else— maybe Bonnie or Ben, or someone Mandy fell in love with? He pushed that thought aside.

Maybe, if Drew visited again, she'd even ask him. Like a kid asked a casual acquaintance about things she couldn't ask a parent? He didn't like that thought either. Possible future scenarios whirled and twisted in Drew's head so much that he was surprised to find himself automatically turning into the ranch.

"Thanks for driving us." Mandy scooted out of her seat and opened Ella's door.

"I'll carry her." Drew joined her by the rear passenger door, unbuckled Ella and eased her into his arms. "She's getting too heavy for you."

"'Cause I'm fat?" Ella asked, eyes heavy with sleep.

"No. You're just right," he said without even thinking about it.

"Are you sure?" She yawned.

"Positive. Why?" Strange how right the warmth of her in his arms felt.

"'Cause Bobby Tindal said I wouldn't win the blue ribbon for the race at school because I'm too fat."

"Bobby Tindal is wrong." A sprig of irritation at the unknown boy sprouted, startling Drew with its intensity. "Anyway, winning a blue ribbon for a race isn't such a big deal. You do lots of other things really well." He mounted the stairs and carried her into her room. Smiling at her huge yawn, he set her gently on the bed.

"But I don't have a blue ribbon an' I want one," Ella pouted as she curled on the bed, already half asleep.

"I'll get you one, Bella Ella," he whispered, compelled to brush his lips against her cheek.

"G'night Drew. I love you." She smiled when he didn't immediately respond. "An' you love me," she said. And then she was gone, back to her whiffling snores.

"I should have taken off that dress before she went back to sleep," Mandy fussed. "If I try now, I'll have to wake her up again."

"Forget it. Let her sleep. I'll buy her another dress." A blue ribbon and a new dress. Suddenly aware of what he'd said, uncomfortably mindful that it sounded too familiar, too—fatherly, Drew backed out of the room. "I'd better go. Good night."

"Good night," Mandy called.

Drew walked out the door. He was tired but it wasn't a physical tiredness that could be mended with sleep. It was a mental weariness. Why was he here? What was he supposed to do about this child Mandy insisted was his daughter?

Better yet, what was he supposed to do about Mandy? He knew his parents believed he owed her marriage, but that wasn't going to happen. For one thing, Mandy would never agree to it. She loved working the ranch. For the past year and a half, she'd made this place Ella's home. Drew needed the city. That was his home, or it would become so someday. Hopefully.

Even if he did stay, which was impossible, Ella, not to mention the whole community of Sunshine, would eventually figure out he was her father. Then Ella's questions about daddies and his role in her life would balloon. It was already difficult. Add people's hints and ceaseless gossip, and it could hurt Ella. Never mind that acknowledging his fatherhood but not really being Ella's father would disrupt the security Mandy had so carefully created for her daughter.

Drew was in an untenable situation, and for the first time in his life, he couldn't just walk away from it.

The night was warm, the wind light, so he walked the ranch, trying to sort out the miasma of confusion that whirled inside, struggling to decipher the spreadsheet that was his incomprehensible future.

Odd how all the high spots included Mandy and Ella.

Chapter Seven

"I'm sad we can't go camping this summer, Mama."

"So am I, sweetheart. But with Auntie Bonnie and Uncle Ben in the hospital, I have to stay here and look after the ranch for them until they're better." Mandy didn't add that she had no idea how much time that might take.

"'Cause we love them." Ella nodded before biting a chunk out of her slice of watermelon. She lifted her face to the sun as juice dribbled down her chin, her sunny smile back in place. "I love picnics. An' I love you."

"I love you, too, sweetheart." Mandy dabbed away the sticky mess and tried not to think about the hundred or so things she should be doing on the ranch. Time with Ella was more important than anything else. That's what Bonnie and Ben would tell her.

"You two look comfy."

Mandy startled. She hadn't even heard Drew ride up.

"May I join you?" he asked, waiting for her nod before he dismounted and looped his horse's reins around a branch. "That looks yummy."

"It is." Ella held out the container of fruit when he sat beside her. "You get messy eating waterlemon." She giggled when juice ran down his chin.

"Watermelon," Mandy corrected.

"S'what I said." Ella grinned. "Mama will have to clean you up."

"Will she?"

The curious hint underlying that question and the look in Drew's dark eyes sent a shiver through Mandy. Was he flirting with her?

"How did today's ride go?" she asked, desperate to get the focus off of her.

"Oh, great!" Drew's droll tone and his nose wrinkled in disgust said it all. "Two kids fell off their horses, one ate a bug and the other was sick all over me. I had to take a dip in the creek, which is colder than an iceberg, I might mention, to get rid of the stench. Talk about fun afternoons."

"What kind of a bug was it?" Ella asked, eyes wide with curiosity.

"Not the kind meant for eating, kiddo. Don't try it." Drew chuckled at her disappointment.

"But, Drew…" Mandy hesitated, a worried frown marring her beauty.

"Don't look like that, Manda Panda. Everyone is fine," Drew assured her. "Oliver told one of Ben's goofy stories, with a few embellishments, and the kids left laughing."

Manda Panda, her old nickname that only Drew had ever used, revived a host of memories Mandy didn't want to revive.

"Who's Manda Panda?" Ella's eyes stretched wide. "Mama?"

"When I lived here before, I used to call her that," Drew admitted, dabbing at her wet chin. "Just like I sometimes call you Bella Ella."

"Oh." The little girl thought about it for a moment before excitement had her jumping up. "Can I go swimming, Mama?" Her face shone. "I love swimming."

"I know you do, honey. Maybe next week or the week after. Remember Drew said it was really cold? When it warms up a little more, you can try the creek, as long as I'm with you." She added the last as a warning because recently Ella had become bolder and more adventurous. It was natural but worrying all the same.

Mandy had planned this afternoon with relaxation in mind. Now she was anything but. Every time this man came near, she tensed up. Because she expected something bad to happen?

"What did you eat for lunch on the trail ride, Drew?" Ella asked. Her daughter found an interest in every subject.

"Hot dogs."

"That's not all there was to eat," Mandy reminded him.

"No." Drew shrugged. "There was other stuff. But mostly I concentrated on the hot dogs. With pickles and onions and mustard. Oh, and there was dessert. Brownies. My favorite."

"Yum. That makes me want some." Ella patted her stomach. "We ate sandwiches and waterlemon. It was good, but I want something else."

"There's lots of fruit," Mandy pointed out hopefully. Once Ella got an idea, she didn't let go.

"Unless I eat the last piece," Drew teased.

"How come we didn't bring brownies, Mama?" Ella's expressive face revealed her disappointment.

"I brought an afternoon snack we could share. If your mother says it's okay," Drew added belatedly after Mandy cleared her throat.

"What is it?" Mandy nodded when he held out two chocolate bars. "I guess something sweet would be okay." She sipped from her thermal cup.

"Is that coffee?" Drew asked, eyes wide.

"Yes. Why?" Mandy didn't like the way his gaze narrowed.

"I'll share my treats with you," he said slowly, pretending he was talking to Ella, "on one condition."

"What's a con-dition?" Ella tipped her head to one side like a curious bird.

"I'll share with you if you share something with me," he explained.

"I already did!" Ella grinned. "Our fruit. 'Member?"

"Something else." Drew stared at Mandy, his gaze dark and penetrating.

"He wants to trade for my coffee, honey." Ella had seen the chocolate bars. There was no going back now. Mandy held out her cup. "Take it."

"No, Mama. You said you needed your coffee so we could hike to the lookout." Ella glared at Drew. "I don't want any chocolate," she said, then added almost belligerently, "Thank you."

Drew stared at her as if he couldn't believe what he was hearing. Mandy was surprised, too. Ella had willingly given up her favorite treat to allow her mother to enjoy *her* favorite thing. The sweet gesture brought tears to her eyes.

"It's okay, sweetie. You have the chocolate and Drew can have the coffee. I've had enough," she reassured her.

But Ella stubbornly shook her head.

"No, thank you." She started packing her saddle bag. "Can we go now, Mama?" She avoided looking at Drew.

Mandy saw the confusion on Drew's face and knew he was struggling to understand. She wasn't sure she did either.

"What's wrong, honey?"

"I don't like con-con-ditions," Ella said, chin thrust out. "People should share with each other with no con-ditions, 'specially people who love each other." She gathered the reins of her pony. "Let's go, Mama." She ignored Drew completely.

"Honey, Drew didn't mean—"

"Yes, I did, Manda Panda. And Ella knows it." Drew squatted in front of the little girl. "I'm sorry, Bella Ella.

You're right. Friends share without conditions." He held out his hand. "I apologize."

"'S'okay." Ella studied him for a moment before thrusting out her own hand to shake his. "But I don't want any chocolate now 'cause we gotta go afore it gets too late. Auntie Bonnie said you never ever be at Big Rock when it's dark."

"She's absolutely right. May I join you, Ella?" Drew's humble request shocked Mandy.

"Sure." Ella's sunny smile was back.

He must be really bored if he wanted to join them on a hike to a place he'd been to a hundred times before. But Mandy said nothing as she waited for Ella to mount up and then followed suit. They moved across the meadow silently. Ella seemed content to savor the beauty of the blooming wildflowers around her. As she meandered ahead, Drew pulled his horse next to Mandy's.

"It's good you can find time to ride with Ella," he said quietly.

"What does that mean?" Mandy whirled to face him, startling her horse so she had to calm him. "You think I'm slacking off?"

"Hey, I didn't say that." Drew's lips pursed. "Stop reading ulterior motives into my every word."

"They're usually there," she muttered, not quite under her breath, eyes on Ella who was about fifty yards ahead.

"I just meant I'm glad you two can share time together." Drew's brow furrowed as his gaze rested on their daughter. "You told me when I first came here that Ella had learning disabilities, which I think, after getting to know her, must be minimal. But I'm curious. Was she born with them?"

"Her birth was problematic." Immediately guilt rushed in.

She'd asked for forgiveness, given up even the idea of love and being loved. Why wasn't that enough? Mandy so didn't want to go back to that dark place and those painful memories. Drew would hate her when he knew—

"Problematic. What does that mean exactly?" he pressed.

"I had to have surgery. They told me Ella had trouble catching her first breath."

So not the whole story, but Mandy was nowhere near ready to bare her heart and reveal her guilty past. Rejection was the likeliest outcome, and she couldn't deal with that right now.

"So...?" Drew kept a bead on her.

"The doctors believe that caused some brain damage which is revealed in several ways. One of them is learning issues," she offered when Drew kept his gaze on her.

"Oh." Silence for a few moments, then, "I'm sorry."

"So am I." Mandy shrugged. "But she's improving and she's become much better since we moved here. Less inclined to outbursts, probably because she feels comfortable with the same people around all the time. Or so I'm told."

"But there are strangers coming and going at the ranch all the time," he protested.

"There are. However, the main people in her world besides me—Bonnie, Ben and Trina—are constants. Her preschool is a constant." She shrugged. "Anyway, that's what her psychologist says is helping."

"Psychologist? That has to be expensive." Drew whistled.

"It is. Very. I'm grateful my health plan covers it, and this psychologist is worth every penny." Mandy searched desperately for an alternative subject.

"Come on, Mama! Hurry!" Ella bellowed, her eyes wide with excitement.

"Coming." Mandy nudged her horse with her knees and trotted toward her daughter. "How come you're so impatient today?"

"I wanna pick wildflowers up there," Ella muttered as she slid off her pony and pointed to the craggy peak towering above them. "I'm gonna get Auntie Bonnie's favorite an' take them to her an' Uncle Ben next time we go."

"But the flowers will wilt—"

"Auntie Bonnie told me she's missing her wildflowers," Ella insisted, a determined set to her chin that reminded Mandy of Drew. "She was sad."

"Then we must pick her some wildflowers and cheer her up," her father agreed. "We have to walk from here, right?" At Mandy's nod, Drew tied his and Ella's horses loosely to the branch of a tree. He raised one eyebrow, obviously waiting for her to do the same. "Another headache?" he guessed quietly when she rubbed the throbbing spot on her forehead. "Do you get them often?"

"I'm fine." How did he notice things like that? It was almost as if he was inside her head. Vowing to be less transparent, Mandy dismounted, tied the horse and shouldered the pack she always carried on her trips with Ella. "Ready?" she asked her daughter.

"Uh-huh." Ella fastened her hat under her chin and stepped forward confidently toward the path that led up to the rocky promontory known as Big Rock. "Did you bring the camera, Mama? I want to text Aunt Bonnie a picture, too."

"I have my phone. We'll use that." Ella took a step forward but Mandy stopped her. "I go first, honey. Like we always do," she added as a reminder. "You go next, then Drew can follow. Okay?" She glanced at him for confirmation.

"Good by me." Drew nodded.

As her daughter launched into an off-key chorus she'd learned at church, Mandy stepped onto the path and surreptitiously scanned her surroundings. On a ride near here a week ago, she'd found signs that a bear with cubs had been in the area. As usual, she'd brought her spray and whistle. She'd encountered the animals before and scared them away, so she wasn't worried. Just on the lookout.

"It's unlikely there's any creature lurking within a mile given Ella's uh, singing," Drew murmured in her ear.

"Maybe." She tilted her head to look at him and felt a shiver of awareness sift through her along with—what? A wishful hope for something that could never be? Suddenly conscious that she was staring, Mandy hastily moved forward to catch up to her daughter who had rushed past them both, eager to collect her precious flowers.

"We can sit here, Mama," Ella called.

"Ella, wait." Mandy climbed faster, slipped and finally ascended the top. Drew passed her as she bent to check her scraped knee while mentally preparing a rebuke for her daughter.

"Ella…" Something in Drew's breathless whisper made Mandy look.

She froze, terror gripping her. Ella stood teetering on the craggy edge of a promontory, loose stones beneath her shoes. Vivid cracks showed along the edge, no doubt due to the drought they were experiencing.

Oh, Lord, help!

"Isn't it pretty, Mama?" Ella waved a hand to encompass the valley laid out before them. A pebble broke free beneath her foot and tumbled down into the vast space. She barely noticed. "Like a picture."

A dangerous picture that could send her daughter hurtling down the hillside any moment.

Mandy met Drew's gaze and gulped. She felt encased in ice, unable to move, breathe or beg Ella to step back. For once she had to depend on him because all she could do was silently pray.

"Ella, I want you to step backward two steps." Drew's hoarse tone betrayed his own fear.

"Like in a game?" Ella asked gaily. She turned slightly to grin at him, inadvertently sending a rock shower down the precipice.

"Stop!" Drew cleared his throat when Ella stared at him uncertainly. "Yes, Bella Ella." His voice altered, grew softer, more coaxing. "Exactly like in a game. The game is, you can't take a step unless I say, *Mama says*. If I say, *take a step* and I don't say *Mama says*, you can't do it. Okay?"

"I don't like games." Ella could sense something wasn't right. Her eyes searched her father's before she looked at Mandy.

"You'll be really good at this game, sweetheart." Mandy forced herself to sound unconcerned, even happy. "It's an easy one. I'm going to play, too. Okay, Drew?"

"Sure. It's always better if there are more people. Okay, Ella, Mama says, take one baby step backward. Good," he applauded when, after an unsure pause, she stepped back. "Mandy, take one giant step forward."

"No, Mama!" Ella yelled excitedly when Mandy lifted her foot. "He didn't say Mama says."

"Right." Mandy stayed where she was but tossed a dark glare at Drew. As if this was the time to trick her! But Drew didn't look like he was teasing. He looked as scared as she felt.

"Ella, Mama says take four medium-sized steps backward." Drew waited until Ella had complied. She was almost safely away from the dangerous cliff edge. Almost. He sent Mandy moving right, toward her daughter. "Good. Now Ella, take six giant steps backward. Mama says," he added quickly.

"I can only take five," the little girl protested when she bumped into her mother and they both collapsed onto the ground. Ella gave the white-faced man a dubious look before whispering, "I don't think Drew knows this game very good, Mama."

"Very well," Mandy corrected automatically. "I think he knows it just fine, baby." She wrapped her arms around her child and hung on while offering a silent prayer of thanks.

"You win, Ella. Good game." Drew high-fived the smiling child.

Mandy released her daughter, her heart brimming with relief.

"Thank you," she said to Drew when Ella was safely picking the wildflowers far back from the crag. "That was a smart move."

"Instinct. I think I just aged ten years." He raked a hand through his hair. "How is it that you're not yet gray?"

"Hair color," she teased. "Seriously, thank you. I don't know what I'd have done if you hadn't been here."

"You'd have figured out something. I'm sure this isn't the first time Ella's needed rescuing." He sagged wearily. "I doubt it will be the last."

"On that cheerful thought, let's take a break by this tree." Mandy dared Drew to argue as she insisted, "You brought chocolate bars and I want half of one. Now. I need the sugar. You can have what's left of my coffee. Maybe it will revive you."

"I doubt it, but thanks. I accept." Drew took the thermos from her, unfastened the top and poured the last few ounces of the coffee into it. "I follow the package directions to the letter, but my coffee never tastes like this. Never," he added mournfully after the first sip. He closed his eyes, obviously enjoying the hit of caffeine. "I have never been so afraid in my entire life."

"Really?" Mandy blinked. "You didn't look as terrified as I felt. My jaws locked and I couldn't let out the scream inside."

"Good thing you didn't. Ella might have stepped over the edge. Although I have to say…" He paused, brows furrowed as he thought it over. "I have never seen anyone as sure-footed as she is. Or maybe nimble is the word."

"It took a while for Ella to learn to walk like that. She bumped into stuff and fell down for eons until a neighbor, a former ballet dancer, taught her to walk gracefully with her back straight, like gliding, only she called it moonwalking. She coaxed Ella to do exercises to music, which strengthened her muscles. Ella loved it."

"Nice lady," Drew murmured.

"A gift from God when I truly needed one." A rush of pride filled Mandy. "Ella practiced faithfully day after day. She slowly learned how to carefully place her feet for each step just like Miss Grace." She smiled at the memory. "Those lessons are engraved in her brain, just like our days with Miss Partridge are."

"Oh, why did you have to mention her? I'd just begun to recover." Drew sagged against the tree, his expression grimly comical. "This morning, before I left with the group, she told me my seat was off, that I'd lost my posture position. As if!"

Mandy hid her grin behind her hand, pretending to cough as she watched Ella choose the very best wildflowers for her bouquet for Bonnie.

"Actually," he mused, "it sounded like something you'd say to those teenage girls who come to train for riding in formations." His gaze narrowed.

"I did say something like that to Miss Partridge at her riding lesson this morning. She obviously practiced it to tell someone else." Mandy couldn't stop her laughter when he glowered. "Get over it. She's a lonely old lady with a heart of gold who—"

"Has a tongue like a sword," Drew finished with a growl.

"And a brain just as sharp. Don't do anything to set her off," Mandy warned. "Or she'll start looking for something to tell the world about us. And don't ask her any questions. You know how she loves to show off her encyclopedic memory."

"Good to know years of taxpayer dollars are being put to good use," he grumbled, then grimaced. "Sorry, that's cranky of me."

"Very." She ducked her head, noted his face seemed whiter than normal when he studied Ella. "What's the matter?"

"This parenting thing." Drew's voice had a ragged edge. "Not that I will ever be one," he assured her, barely meeting her gaze before looking away. "Today just proved that. How do you survive it, Mandy? One afternoon and I feel like I've just suffered a major heart attack."

"It's not like this every day," Mandy said, a rush of sympathy swelling. "Most kids are curious. They like to explore. With Ella, I've encouraged that, but I also try to ensure she understands that there are boundaries and that she'll face consequences if she deliberately breaks the rules. Today I wasn't clear enough, I guess."

"She didn't realize she was in danger," he whispered in amazement, watching as Ella danced in the flower meadow, swaying from side to side, arms outstretched as if she was floating. "I'm actually glad about that."

"You are?" Mandy watched him nod. "Why?"

"Because I remember being afraid when I first moved here," Drew said, his voice harsh. "I was terrified of everything, especially that I'd be left alone again."

Mandy kept silent, sensing he needed to say this.

"I was awake after the accident. I knew when my parents didn't answer me that they were gone. My brothers weren't conscious either." Drew exhaled heavily. "I was alone for what seemed like hours. I had nightmares about it for a long time. I don't ever want Ella to feel like I did."

"You never told me about any nightmares." Proof positive that she had never really known Drew?

"I never told anyone. I made myself get over it." He said the words stiffly, as if it hurt to admit.

Suddenly Mandy understood. That nine-year-old boy had made himself get over it by learning how to survive as a loner. Only he'd never really gotten over it at all. Sadness gripped Mandy for that traumatized child who was now a man but who was still afraid.

"Do you think that soon Ella will stop asking me if I'm going to be her daddy?" Drew's quiet question broke through her thoughts.

"I doubt it." Mandy had to be honest because it might help him, show him he needed to keep some distance between his daughter and himself if he was not going to pursue the relationship.

Pursue the relationship? Get real, Mandy.

Wasn't it about time to stop hoping and praying, even pretending to herself that something might change Drew's mind, at least about being a father to Ella?

Chapter Eight

"I need Thursday evenings off, starting this week."

A few days later Mandy blinked, surprised to see Drew standing in the doorway of her office, but even more surprised by his request.

"Okay," she agreed after a glance at the wall schedule. "Doesn't look like it's a problem until the last week of June." She made a note.

"By which time I'll probably be gone." He nodded, pushed back his Stetson. "Thanks." Her curiosity must have revealed itself on her face because he snickered. "Go ahead. Ask me."

"None of my business," she said and bent to recheck her latest computer entry.

"Guess anyway," he said, his voice lighthearted.

Playful Drew. She hadn't seen this side of him since—never mind.

"I have some accounting to do, Drew. It's not the best time—" Mandy bit her lip. Maybe if she just played along, he'd leave quicker and she'd be able to breathe again.

"Work," she guessed, but she knew her response came too late from the way his eyes lit up at the word accounting.

"Wrong. I'm joining John Purdy's men's Bible study." He chuckled at her surprise. "Courtesy of Oliver. Miss

Partridge suggested to him that I might enjoy their men's group. Do you think I have to thank her?" He made a face.

"Yes, because that is a special group of men. Enjoy it." Mandy bent her head, hoping he'd take the hint and leave. As if.

"Did I see Jeff Sanderson in here earlier?" Drew's scrutiny was intense.

"Yes." She laid down her pencil. "Turns out I owe him a big apology."

"Because?" One imperious eyebrow arched as if he highly doubted that.

"Turns out he really does want to have dinner with me," she began, holding up a hand to forestall his interruption, "to discuss my thoughts on an appropriate and memorable gift for his wife after the birth of their child."

"Oh." Drew blinked.

"Oh, indeed. Shame on me for thinking bad thoughts about him." Mandy huffed out a breath that blew her bangs awry. "Now, please excuse me. I need to get back to work."

"What're you doing?" Drew pulled up a chair, sat down beside her uninvited and grinned. "Excel. I'm impressed."

"Don't be. It's still my least favorite program," she grumbled.

"Meaning you're still no good at the formulas." He studied the screen. "Dare I ask what you're trying to do?"

Mandy exhaled. Clearly Drew wasn't going away just yet.

"Ben has always lumped supply costs together, but I want to keep separate spreadsheets for different operational facets of the ranch," she told him, secretly grateful that he'd come along and was willing to help. If there was one thing Drew knew, it was spreadsheets.

But his proximity made her nervous. *Businesslike*, she reminded herself.

"You even want to track the guests' meal costs?" he asked, his surprise obvious.

"Everything. If we know where the money's going, we can be more mindful about how we spend it." Mandy pointed out what she'd created so far. "I also want to split off the vet bills for each animal, see which ones repeatedly need treatment. Maybe we're missing something that we could do to cut back on their medical needs."

"Very smart," he agreed, eyes wide with what Mandy hoped was new respect. He studied the computer, then doused the bit of pleasure she'd found. "This isn't going to work."

He tried to explain why, but Mandy had neither the time nor the patience to grasp the finer points of his argument.

"Just leave me to work on it, Drew. I can get it if I keep at it—oh!" She gasped as her carefully built columns and the information they contained disappeared. "Oh no! That took me forever and now it's gone. What a waste of time!"

"It's not gone. Move over." Drew growled when she remained in place. "Do you want me to fix this, or not, Mandy? Decide quickly because I have to guide that kids' choral group shortly. What's your answer?"

"Yes," she said, giving in despite her reservations about having him so close. As she slid her chair to the side, her arm brushed his and her breath caught.

"All rightie then." Obviously excited, Drew jubilantly cracked his knuckles, bent over the computer and began tapping. Moments later her numbers reappeared, but in a different format. He minimized that and with a few more taps had a completely new form on the screen, complete with the ranch's logo on top.

"How did you—?" Mandy's heart bumped clear down to her stomach when Drew turned his head and flashed his knee-knocking grin.

"This is what I do, Manda Panda," he said, smirking

like his ten-year-old self. "I build spreadsheets for analysis." He winked. "And I'm really, really good at it."

"Yes, you are," she agreed softly, stupidly proud of his abilities when she had no right to be.

"Okay, so this will be your new form for keeping track of supplies." Drew explained the columns he'd created.

"I need a bunch of forms because we have a lot of horses," she pointed out.

"This is your template. I've labeled it Blank. Every time you want to start a new file for a different horse, you'll replace Blank with the horse's name and save it in a brand new expense file. We'll put that in a subfile for horses, which then goes in the big file called Expenses. You can have a subfile for cattle, one for the petting zoo, even one for garden produce if you want. Okay?" He looked at her expectantly.

"Um, I already have an expense file."

"Yes, but it doesn't contain all the other information you want. This will." Drew's delight made it impossible not to return his smile. This was the happiest he'd looked since he'd arrived. "I'll show you. Let's take a horse. Raven, for example. She's probably got the most medical bills."

He entered the information, then again explained how to save the files in distinct categories. In minutes he'd created an entry page for every one of the Double H's horses.

"It's great, Drew. I can't thank you enough," Mandy said dutifully.

"I hear a *but*." He leaned back and waited.

"But I'll have to reenter everything I've already entered in my old system. It will take me forever and I haven't got that much free time right now." Mandy didn't need to say computers were her least favorite thing about ranch work. Drew already knew that.

"Merging should be pretty easy…" He dove into her

files and studied them intensely, apparently unaware that his knee kept bumping hers.

Mandy's stomach sank when he finally pushed away from the desk. "No good?"

"Your programs are really old, Mandy, you haven't used the same format for all of the files and some of them files are corrupted. I don't use merging much in my work but transferring everything should be doable. I just need a bit of time to do it. Thing is, I have to leave now to take my singers' group." He rose, picked up his hat and put it on, dark eyes thoughtful. "I've saved it. I'll take another look later on this evening. Everything's password protected, right?"

"Yes. I use Ella's birth date." She rattled it off before realizing exactly what details she was revealing to him.

The significance of those dates impacted Drew like an ice storm. He froze. Was he, too, remembering those last moments they'd shared?

"So Ella really is my daughter," he said in a tight voice, his former easygoing manner completely gone.

"I already told you that." Mandy didn't say anything else because she sensed there was a struggle happening inside his head.

"Yes, you did." He scrutinized her for several long moments before wheeling around and walking toward the door. "I have to go."

"Thank you for the help." His reaction puzzled Mandy. "See you later," she called to his retreating back. She shrugged at his nonresponse and tried to continue working. But the memory of that stark awareness dawning in Drew's eyes would not dissipate.

Now that he had Ella's birth date, would it change anything?

"Don't get your hopes up, girlfriend," she chided herself. "Learning that date doesn't mean that Drew suddenly wants to be a daddy."

"Drew wants to be a daddy?" Ella stood in the doorway. "My daddy?" she asked with wide-eyed hopefulness.

Lord, when will I learn to shut up?

"Sweetie, I didn't say that," Mandy rushed to correct herself. "Drew doesn't want to be a daddy to anyone. He lives by himself in a big city." Tears welled in Ella's eyes but Mandy had to end her futile hope. "I don't think he has room for anyone in his life, sweetheart."

And isn't that the truth, Manda Panda?

"Where's your head at, Drew?" Oliver chided as they built a campfire for the youth group they were escorting. "A couple of times during that ride I was afraid you were going to lead us into the wild blue yonder and right over a cliff."

"Sorry. Guess I'm a little distracted," Drew apologized. Apparently his plan to carry on as if nothing had changed wasn't working.

"A little? Let me guess. You and Mandy argued again." Oliver's eyes widened when Drew shook his head. "Then what's wrong?"

"Just—life." He didn't know how to explain that the combined knowledge of Ella's birth date and the absolutely unavoidable certainty that he was her father had knocked him completely off-kilter.

"Anything I can help with?" Oliver was obviously curious. "Want to sound off to me? It wouldn't go beyond us."

"Thanks, but—I'm not sure that would help." Drew scrambled for a way to express his jumbled mess of conflicting feelings. "Did you ever know something, sort of, but then the truth of it hit you out of the blue and knocked your whole world off balance?"

"Hmm. Not sure if I understand that." Oliver squeezed

his eyes closed for a second, then said, "Let's see. Someone told you something was true and you had no reason to doubt them, but you kind of did—until you didn't? Close?"

"Actually—yeah." Drew stared at his coworker with new appreciation. "That's exactly what's happened."

"And now the truth of what they said has been proven and it's knocked you back on your heels so far that you're not sure what to do about it," the cowboy continued.

"Bang on," Drew agreed. "I feel—"

"Gobsmacked." Oliver chuckled at his surprise. "What? You think I don't know words? An English friend introduced me to the meaning of that word eons ago and trust me, it fits a lot of situations."

"Don't I know it? Gobsmacked is exactly how I felt when Mandy first asked me to come back here." Drew laid the last log on the fire, checked that it wouldn't tumble off and straightened. "The kids are ready to start their meeting here. Let's see if they left us anything to eat."

"I'm down with that." Oliver laughed out loud. "I'm also cool and hip and any other descriptor you've got, though at the moment I am definitely not gobsmacked."

"Oh, brother." Drew made a face when Oliver swayed his hips as he walked to the chuck wagon.

The men sat a distance away from the now-singing group, contentedly eating as the echo of voices performing scales rang around them. Then they helped pack up the wagon so it could be returned, making certain the s'mores ingredients stayed behind.

"Don't know why they need s'mores," Oliver grumbled as he munched on oatmeal cookies. "There was enough dessert on that wagon to stuff 'em full."

"They're kids. As I recall, Bonnie baked nonstop and I ate nonstop at that age." Drew cupped his iced tea glass in his palms and listened to the melodic voices echoing around the valley. "Though I freely admit I know less than nothing about kids," he added.

"Everybody starts out that way. Like me. Confirmed bachelor till I came to Hanging Hearts Ranch." Oliver grinned. "But I learned pretty fast that kids are as terrified of messing up as I am."

"Maybe." Drew doubted anyone could mess up as badly as he had. "This group sounds amazing."

"They come here every year, right before their big singing competition in Missoula. Their director says singing out here amplifies where they're off-key so well that the kids can hear it for themselves." He scratched his head. "Or something like that. I don't always understand when she starts talking music."

"Well I for one do not hear anything off-key." Drew closed his eyes as the singers moved into a quiet, evocative piece about listening for God's voice. He glanced at Oliver. "Do you think that's really possible?"

"What? Hearing God?" Oliver nodded as he packed their utensils for transport. "I do."

"How? Like a voice in a bush?" Drew wasn't trying to mock. He was serious.

"I'm no Moses." Oliver shrugged. "I think God uses more subtle means to speak to us these days. I mean a voice in the bush would draw network television and then whatever He was trying to tell us would be lost in the hubbub."

"So how does God talk specifically, personally?" Drew voiced the question that had haunted him for years, hoping his new friend had an answer.

"Psalms tells us to be still and know God," Oliver said quietly. "I think that means an inner knowledge, or a prompting that we sense nudging us in a certain direction."

"But how do we get that nudge?" Drew needed to hear Oliver's response.

"By being quiet and listening, by waiting and by tuning out all the noise inside our heads."

"You hear noises in your head?" Drew teased, then sobered when Oliver nodded.

"We all do. The *shoulda, woulda, coulda* voices are in my head constantly, making me feel bad. Likewise, the guilt voices and the fear voices." Oliver grinned. "You look shocked."

"Because I can't fathom you afraid of anything." Drew so wanted to hear Oliver's answers, even though asking made him feel foolish. The darkening sky lent some privacy to their conversation, which helped.

"That's one thing I figured out through our Bible studies," Oliver reflected. "Even the biggest, burliest guy is afraid of something. I'm afraid I'll lose another kid."

"You had a child?" Drew sank onto a nearby boulder, stunned. "But you said—"

"It wasn't my child. It was someone else's, which makes it worse." He squeezed his eyes closed as if it was too painful to talk about.

"I don't want to pry," Drew murmured.

"You're not prying. Besides, I'm told that talking about it is good for me." Oliver didn't look up. His voice became a low rumble that Drew had to lean in to hear. "I used to be a teacher. We took our kids on field trips before school finished for the year. The seventh graders I taught wanted to go white-water rafting. We did and one of them, a girl, died."

"I'm sorry." Drew figured the child must have drowned. "Kids should have to take swimming lessons really young."

"Anna didn't drown. When our bus broke down, it took a while to get help. She went into diabetic shock." The emptiness of Oliver's voice revealed his pain. "I couldn't save her."

"But that wasn't your fault, Ollie. She should have brought extra insulin or something," Drew defended his friend.

"It *was* my fault. I wanted to show the kids a certain plant species so I took a detour through some rough terrain. That's why the bus broke down. It was my fault Anna died." He lifted his head and stared at Drew, his round face shiny with tears. "I never taught again after that, couldn't take the risk that I'd be the cause of some other kid's death or injury."

"That's understandable." Drew felt sorry for this man, yet he'd consistently marveled at Oliver's great rapport with kids who came to the ranch. "I felt like that for years after our parents were killed in the car accident that injured my brothers and me. Guilty. I lived and my parents died. To this day, despite Bonnie and Ben's best efforts, I still don't feel like the Double H is home, that it will ever compare to the home I lost that day."

"Why does this home have to compare to the other one?" Oliver frowned. "And why was it up to Ben and Bonnie to make it that way?"

"I—I don't know. Because they wanted to be my parents?" Drew gaped at the other man. "I'm not sure what you're getting at."

"A home isn't something someone gives you, Drew." The big cowboy leaned back against a tree, his words slow and thoughtful. "A home is created by people who join together for their common good, blood-related or not. It's not a place that's waiting for you to arrive," he added.

"Huh?" Drew didn't get it.

"You *make* your home by contributing, by giving and by sharing with people you care about. Maybe that's why you never felt comfortable here, because you didn't invest anything of yourself into making this place your home."

"But—" Drew stopped, gulped. Something about Oliver's comment rang true.

"Maybe you never 'let' yourself belong here because it would have meant opening yourself to loving and possibly losing again." Oliver shrugged. "After I quit teaching, I wouldn't let myself take a risk. I think you're the same. That's why you're standoffish with the kids who come here, so they won't get too close."

"I'm not standoffish," Drew protested.

"Sure you are." Oliver's big grin eased the sting of his words. "Because if you don't get too involved, you won't do anything that can hurt them or you. Am I wrong?" he pressed when Drew didn't answer.

Drew wouldn't, couldn't respond because he was stuck wondering if his riding buddy had just revealed a truth about him.

"The issue is self. It's always about self and our concept of who we are. In my case I had to realize that life wasn't all about me, what I wanted or needed. Before I figured that out, I became so unhappy that I ran away." Oliver made a face. "Avoiding the hard stuff was my standard operating procedure."

Mine, too, Drew thought.

"I went over the side of a cliff. Not purposely, but I got stuck there, couldn't get out of my car. There was no way to avoid facing what I'd become, to see myself as God sees me. A taker." Oliver looked ashamed. "That's when I figured out that life isn't about getting. It's about giving, being involved, helping, doing anything I can to make the world better for other people. Because doing that makes the world better for me."

"I see." Maybe it had worked for Oliver, but Drew didn't think getting more involved than he already was would help anyone. He wasn't the warm and fuzzy type.

"Ben was a member of the rescue team that found me two days later. He offered me a job here and—voilà!" He spread his hands. "Here I am. Hanging Hearts Ranch is my home. My life has never been better since I took the focus off myself and put it on other people. But I had to *make* this place my home. That took an active role on my part. I didn't just walk in here and find someone had made a home ready and waiting for me." He snickered. "I wouldn't have appreciated that anyway. Working out the kinks of fitting in here is what *makes* Hanging Hearts Ranch my home."

The singing group was ready to roast marshmallows for their s'mores. There was no more time for talk. Drew tucked away what he'd learned, vowing to reexamine what Oliver had said later, when he was alone.

I had to make this place my home.

Like Mandy had?

Chapter Nine

"Happy Mother's Day."

"Thanks." Mandy gulped as she accepted the gigantic bouquet from Drew, who stood on her doorstep. She wasn't exactly sure how to deal with him these days. On one hand, she liked that they weren't arguing as much anymore. It was far too busy for that.

On the other hand, she worried.

Drew seemed to go out of his way to spend more time with Ella, and from what her daughter let slip, some of their time together was spent discussing Ella's early childhood. Mandy wasn't happy about that, fearing Drew would ask her to fill in the blanks.

The last thing she wanted to do was go back, to feel the overwhelming guilt billow once more, to let him know she'd cost him much more than he knew.

"Can I catch a ride to church again?" Drew asked, one eyebrow arched. "Bonnie's car is at the garage. New tires."

"Oh." Mandy swallowed. "Yes, sure. We'll be ready in half an hour or so."

"It's potluck day again, isn't it? Mother's Day luncheon?" There was an odd gleam of anticipation in those dark eyes that suggested Drew might even be looking forward to going to church. "Are you planning on staying?"

"Yes. I couldn't talk Ella out of it." Only after she'd said it did Mandy realize how unhappy she sounded. "I was hoping to see Aunt Bonnie today, do something special for her."

"We could still go." He paused for a moment, thinking it over. "What if we took a cake along and had Mother's Day tea with Bonnie and Ben? Ella would love it. She's always up for a tea party. Ma would like it, too."

"Sure. That sounds nice." Was this the same Drew of the flowers-and-a-card-delivered-by-someone-else-but-never-in-person, who was planning something special for Bonnie on Mother's Day?

"Close your mouth, Manda Panda," he teased in a low, amused voice. "It's not that unheard of."

Yes, it was. For Drew. But Mandy didn't say that because she didn't want to cause the big grin stretched across his face to disappear. His smile was something to be cherished.

"I don't have a cake," she murmured.

"I made one last week and froze it." He shrugged off her stare. "Every once in a while I like to bake. I also picked up some party stuff."

"Sounds great." A momentary image of Drew as he might have looked if they'd married, if he'd been there for Ella's birth, filled Mandy's head.

Would he have made a special Mother's Day cake for her?

Like a thunderstorm, other memories of that day swept in and erased her fairy-tale notions. She was *glad* he hadn't been there, glad he didn't know what she'd done, what a terrible mother she'd been.

"Mandy?" Drew was staring at her. "You've gone white. Is something wrong?"

"I'm fine," she said quickly, clinging to the door so her

knees wouldn't give out. "See you in half an hour. And thanks for the flowers."

"Sure." He frowned at her, unmoving even as she closed the door on him.

Mandy thrust the beautiful bouquet in a jug of water. Ella emerged from her room and demanded to know where they'd come from. That engendered unanswerable questions, like when would Drew want to be a daddy and was Mandy ever going to get Ella her very own daddy?

Exasperated and on edge, Mandy finally ordered her daughter to get ready for church. Ella's face crumpled and tears rolled down her cheeks as she turned away.

"Oh, honey, I'm sorry." Mandy gathered her precious daughter in her arms and held her close. "I didn't mean to snap at you."

"I didn't try to do bad, Mama," Ella sobbed.

"You didn't do anything bad, sweetheart." How could she have let her guilt overwhelm her enough to cause Ella pain? Mandy pressed her lips against her daughter's wet cheek. "You didn't do anything wrong. And you made me the most beautiful card. That was so sweet."

"Drew helped me. He said I have the bestest mama so she should have the bestest card." Ella smiled, her sad face gone. "He buyed that pink ribbon for me to use on it 'cause he said you always usta like pink. He tol' me you were really good friends."

"Yes, we were." Mandy tried to think of a way to avoid the questions she knew were coming but couldn't.

"An' you don't argue no more 'cause you're really good friends now, right?" Ella asked, eyes sparkling. "Drew's helpin' you while Auntie Bonnie and Uncle Ben get better."

"Yes." Mandy smoothed her hair. "And he's coming with us to church today so we'd better get ready. Because you know what today is."

"Uh-uh." Ella frowned, her forehead pleated. "Mother's Day?"

"Yes, but it's also your favorite." Mandy's heart brimmed with love for this sweet child. At least God hadn't punished her by taking Ella.

"Potluck day! Again?" Ella whooped for joy at Mandy's nod. Then she stopped and looked at her mother very seriously. "Are we takin' sumthin', Mama? Everybody but us always brings sumthin'," she reminded. "We never stay."

"Today we're staying. And we're bringing a pasta salad and a whole watermelon."

"Yummy." Ella rushed off to get ready.

Mandy poured herself another coffee and then walked outside to sit on the step while she mulled over her latest problem.

"Why so serious?" Drew asked from the shade of a nearby tree.

"You scared the daylights out of me," she protested, brushing spilled coffee drops off her hand.

"Sorry." He shrugged, eyes fixated on her mug. "I'm ready to go so I thought I'd wait here for you and Ella." His eyes widened. "Any coffee left to share?"

"Help yourself." When he returned from getting himself a mug of java, Mandy asked, "Have you even tried to make coffee the way I told you?"

"Three pounds' worth," he assured her. He sat down on the step next to her and inhaled. "It never even smelled like this, let alone tasted good."

"I think you're pretending," she muttered before returning to the problem that dogged her. "What are your thoughts on escorting a hike up to Cragg's Peak?"

"Cragg's Peak?" Drew looked thunderstruck. "I haven't been up there for years. I'm not even sure I could handle it without some preparation. Who's asking for a crazy excursion like that?"

"Bankers. They've been here before. The first time Ben took them to the caves," she explained. "Then they heard about the bald eagles that nested here so they came a second time and made a documentary."

"Suits," Drew scoffed. "They'd never make it up that climb and then I'd be responsible for getting them down, possibly with injuries. No way." He shook his head vigorously to emphasize his refusal.

"These aren't your ordinary bankers, Drew," Mandy murmured. "They've climbed all over the world, including Everest."

"Big shots, spending their money with someone else smoothing their way." His sarcasm dripped.

"Not true. These men specifically plan extreme excursions to raise money or to sponsor awareness to help the environment," Mandy countered. "In this case, they hope to draw attention to a new bill that's being proposed to open thus-far protected areas in Glacier National Park."

Drew's eyes widened.

"Such a bill would certainly benefit Hanging Hearts and getting Ben's name on a promotion like that would be a huge boost to his business," she added. "But those aren't the only reasons."

"I'm listening." His dark eyes held hers as memories of past times hiking Cragg's Peak together cascaded through her mind.

"The amount the men have offered for this trip up Cragg's would go a long way toward paying for renovations at Bonnie and Ben's place." Mandy forced back a tide of longing for those happier days when life seemed fun and she felt loved. "Then perhaps your parents could come home sooner."

"I didn't know that was an option." Drew looked startled.

"One of the nurses mentioned it as a possibility, but

only if we can make things more manageable for them in their own home. No carpet. Doorknobs, faucets, handles must be handicap accessible, the type that they can press to open. Stuff like that." Grateful to be talking about something they could work on together without disagreement, Mandy rose. "Also a ramp for the front door."

"I can pay for some of that," Drew muttered. "We don't have to risk life and limb for some wealthy bankers to cover those costs."

"But wouldn't your parents love to know that their own ranch paid for whatever changes are needed?" she countered. "We don't have to give the bankers an answer right away, but I would strongly suggest you think about it, Drew. At the moment we have space to schedule such a climb for the week Ella's at camp, just after school's over."

"What's so great about then?" He stood on the step below her, which put his eyes level with hers. His proximity made Mandy nervous.

"First, the bankers can manage that date. But it's also preferable because I'm free then and could go along."

"Why would you go?" He looked irritated.

"Because if I went along…" Mandy chose her next words carefully. "If there was an issue, it would be my problem to deal with, not yours."

"You don't trust me to handle problems." Drew's lips tightened.

"Not true." Why hadn't she just set the date and said she was going? She was the boss, after all.

"So you're trying to get me off the hook?" Drew's mocking smile annoyed her. "Are you insinuating I'm a wimp, Mandy?"

"No," she denied hotly. "I'm trying to offer you a way out because I know you don't want to take responsibility for someone else. That's what you said," she reminded him.

"Yeah, but—"

"I'm not going because I don't trust you, Drew. I'd trust you on a climb anywhere, anytime." Oops. Had she actually admitted that aloud? "But I don't want you to feel I'm forcing you to do this."

Drew didn't want to be here. That much hadn't changed. Her private fear was that if things got bad enough, he would leave. And as hard as it was to accept, she wanted him to stay, at least a little longer.

"Ever since that nurse spoke to me, I've been trying to devise a way to pay for the needed renovations. Escorting this group could help." She pursed her lips, trying to focus on the point she was making and not on his handsome face. "It would help a lot."

"I get that," he said.

"If you paid for everything, your parents would worry about paying you back, which defeats the whole point of getting them home and comfortable so they don't have to worry." She held his gaze, willing him to understand. "I doubt a fund-raiser is an option. The townsfolk would love it, but—"

"Ma and Pops would hate it," Drew agreed with a sigh. "Pride. They give to the community. They don't take."

"Exactly. Not from their sons either." Mandy stuffed her hands in her pocket. "Please think it over, will you? Meanwhile, we'd better get to church."

"Yeah." His scrutiny suddenly intensified. "No fancy sundress and spike heels?"

"No."

"You don't need them," he said with an appreciative look. "You look great no matter what you wear. I haven't seen you with your hair up in that style for years."

Actually, he hadn't seen her hair in any style for years, but Mandy let it go, tucking away his compliment for later examination. She'd deliberately chosen flowing white cotton pants and a loose flowery top with flat strappy sandals because she was hoping the plainness of this outfit would erase memories of her last appearance at church.

Not that the other men's responses had bothered her unduly. It had been Drew's sideways looks, when he thought she wouldn't notice, that made her wonder if *he* thought she'd dressed that way specifically for him. They already tiptoed around an electric awareness of each other. Mandy didn't want to add to that.

As for her hair, she'd wound it into a topknot because it would be cooler that way, not to induce any past memories in Drew. Hadn't she?

Not ready to pursue that train of thought and not quite ready to leave, Mandy concentrated on her fingernails.

"Can I ask you something really personal, Mandy?" Drew's indecipherable scrutiny set her nerves even more on edge.

"I guess." What now?

"When you were pregnant, did you have tests that told you about Ella?" He stopped, frowned. "I mean, don't doctors do tests ahead of time that tell them…?"

"I asked them not to tell me the gender of my ba— Ella," Mandy said, loathe to explain anything about that time to him, yet knowing that day would surely arrive.

"Actually, I wondered if you knew before you gave birth that Ella—never mind," he said brusquely. "Forget it. It's none of my business."

Then Mandy understood.

"At no time was there any indication that Ella was anything but a healthy, normal child," Mandy told him tightly, her stomach sinking. "Her learning disabilities weren't noticeable until around her first year."

"Oh." The answer seemed to satisfy Drew but thinking he might probe deeper with even more questions about that time, and desperate not to reveal her painful, guilty secret, Mandy cleared her throat.

"Time to go. I'll get Ella." She raced up the stairs and inside as if she was being pursued. *Oh, Lord, will my mistake always haunt me?* "Sweetheart, where are you?"

"Here." Ella sat on the sofa, a book spread in her lap, a smile stretching her bow-shaped lips. "I'm reading, Mama."

"So you are." Tears welled in Mandy's eyes.

Her precious child. How could Drew not want her? Before Ella could notice, Mandy made an excuse and locked herself in the bathroom, ostensibly to check her makeup.

She stared at herself in the mirror, forcing back tears as the truth slammed into her like a boulder tumbling down from the Rockies.

If Drew couldn't get past their beautiful daughter's imperfections, he would never be the daddy Ella so longed for.

And it was all Mandy's fault. That was why she would never be free to love and be loved again. She'd been given that gift, and she'd ruined it.

The punishment is too heavy, God. Because I still love Drew.

After John Purdy's class, Drew hurried outside to find Oliver and hand over Mandy's car keys. He'd insisted he would drive her to church on Mother's Day for a specific reason, and thankfully she hadn't argued. Instead she'd seemed lost in some problem that dimmed her lovely eyes and left almost invisible traces of tearstains.

Drew wondered what had gone wrong, if her tears were his fault. He hated the thought that he might have hurt this generous woman who poured herself into making his parents' ranch a success. Of course he didn't want to hurt her because they'd once been much more than mere friends, and they now shared a bond through Ella. Drew would never be parentally involved in his daughter's life, but that didn't mean he wanted to see either Ella or Mandy suffering.

He returned to the sanctuary for the morning service and took the empty seat next to Mandy, ignoring Miss Partridge perched in the row behind and her knowing grin as the uplifting music called his attention to worship.

Drew had never been much for church, never felt it truly related to him. And yet in these past few weeks, he'd learned more about the nature of God and what He wanted from His creation than he'd imagined was possible to know.

According to John's lesson this morning, God wanted love. That sounded so easy. Yet thanks to the men's Bible study and John's class, Drew now knew it wasn't easy at all. Love meant giving up everything you wanted and making yourself open, vulnerable, to God's wishes, plans and desires. For Drew, that was impossible.

Risk, vulnerability—in his work, he could calculate the odds, measure that against the value gained and decide if the risk was worth it. But with God? How could he foresee or calculate God's odds or measure the immeasurable? Risking himself in that way would cost the thing he held most dear, self-reliance. And Drew just couldn't put that on the line.

Mandy's nudge made him realize the sermon was over. Everyone was standing. He quickly rose for the benediction. That's when he noticed John walking toward him.

"Hey, Drew." John frowned and shifted as if he was uncomfortable.

"Hey." Confused because this confident man seldom looked uneasy, Drew stayed in place when Mandy excused herself to collect Ella. "Something wrong?"

"I don't exactly know." John lifted his head and stared straight at him. "I've never done this before, but somehow I feel compelled to say something to you."

"Oh. Okay." *What's this about?* "Go ahead."

"It's a verse, actually. From Psalm 121. 'I will lift up mine eyes unto the hills, from whence cometh *my help. My help cometh from the Lord*, which made heaven and earth. He will not suffer thy foot to be moved. *He* that keepeth thee will not slumber.' I hope that helps you, Drew."

Then, with a smile, John left.

My help cometh from the Lord.

"Drew?" Mandy, clasping Ella's hand, frowned at him. "Are you sick? Do you not want to stay for potluck?"

"I'm fine." John's particular emphasis on certain words puzzled Drew. He didn't understand what the other man meant, but there was no time to think about it now. He shoved it to the back of his mind to focus on the surprise he and Oliver had planned.

"Ella's really excited today," Mandy said after their daughter begged to join her friends and raced away the moment her mother agreed. "I'm sure she was yakking during children's church. It's not something to do with you, is it?"

"Me?" Drew shook his head. "Nope. Excuse me. I'm supposed to help serve. You'd better get in line, Mama."

He grinned, savoring her confused expression as he walked away. Though the men of the church were in charge of this potluck, some wives, worried about their husbands' abilities in the kitchen, had provided supermarket salads. Turned out they went perfectly with the hamburgers now being grilled. After asking a blessing on the meal, the pastor insisted mothers go first in the food line.

At the sound of Mandy's laughter, Drew glanced up from pouring lemonade. She looked so beautiful and completely comfortable in her world as a mom. He smothered a rush of envy, knowing he'd never be comfortable being a dad.

"Man, you were supposed to let me in the back door," Oliver grumbled in his ear.

"Sorry. I got busy. You got them here without a problem?" Drew asked anxiously.

"Of course." Oliver rolled his eyes. "Would I mess this up?"

"Never." Drew grinned at his friend, barely able to conceal his anticipation. It wasn't easy to surprise Mandy, but this time he figured he and Oliver just might pull it off. "Okay. Meet you back there."

Oliver slipped away. As unobtrusively as possible, Drew handed off his drink duties to someone else, moved to the rear of the kitchen and opened the door. Oliver had parked Bonnie's car outside. The trunk was open, waiting. Moving as quickly as possible, they carried in their surprise and set everything on a long table to the left of the buffet line.

"Pies, gentlemen?" Of course it would be Miss Partridge who first noticed what they were doing. She scanned the array, then surveyed Oliver and Drew with raised eyebrows. "Lemon, blueberry and, if I'm not mistaken, strawberry rhubarb?"

"And two cheesecakes, Miss Partridge." Oliver's chest swelled.

When they were quickly surrounded by others, Drew felt himself shutting down. He hated being the center of attention, wanted to escape. He should have thought this through.

"You two made all these pies?" someone asked in disbelief. "By yourselves?"

"Drew mostly. I just helped." Oliver grinned and repeated it so many times, Drew began to feel annoyed at the disbelief until a voice he knew so well cut in.

"Well, if you folks want to keep looking, go ahead. Excuse me if I take mine and Ella's now, before it's all gone." Mandy edged her way to the table and selected two slices of lemon pie. "Way to go, guys. What a great Mother's Day gift for all of us." She smiled, but her glance lingered on Drew. "Thank you very much."

For Drew, her smile made suffering through the attention totally worth it. Normal chatter resumed in the hall until his Bible study friends began clapping. Drew felt their applause offered true acceptance.

Did he want that? Yes!

"Trying to make the rest of us look bad, huh?" John chuckled.

"Blame Drew," Oliver insisted. "He's the master pie maker. I just helped."

"I like baking." Relieved when Ella tugged on his pant leg, Drew crouched to her level. "What's up, Bella Ella?"

"Thank you for the 'licious pie, Drew." She flung her arms around him and planted a sticky kiss on his cheek. "I wish you were my daddy."

"Why?" Too aware of the crowd around him, some of whom were probably listening, Drew remained in place, hoping he was hidden from onlookers.

"Then you an' me could make pies together." Ella tipped her head near his ear and whispered, "That's what daddies do, Drew. They have fun with their kids. That's why I want my very own daddy."

Her words hit like a hammer blow to his chest. This sweet child wasn't asking for *things*. She wasn't making impossible demands. All Ella wanted was a father to do things with her. What was wrong with him that he would deny her that?

Yet just the thought of having to be there for her, of failing her every time she needed him, when all she asked for was to be loved—Drew's chest tightened and his breathing caught. He wanted that more than he'd thought possible. But it couldn't be.

"You'll have a daddy one day, Ella," he promised in a broken whisper.

"That's what Mama says, too." She heaved a sigh and unclasped her hands from his neck. "But I dunno if God is gonna ever answer my prayers." She walked away, shoulders drooping.

"Is that all you have to give that darling child, Drew?" Miss Partridge stood next to him as he rose. She tut-tutted in obvious disappointment. "You owe her a lot more."

He was glad she spoke in an undertone, but still. "It's not—"

"Any of my business?" Miss Partridge nodded. "It isn't. Except that I've been praying for you and your little family for so long and it hurts to see you throw away such a wonderful gift because you're afraid. How can God answer that sweet girl's prayer when you won't do your part?"

"I can't—"

"Never mind." She shook her head at him mournfully, then added, "But I do thank you for the pies. Giving like this shows you're a part of our church family."

Drew stared at Miss Partridge as she left bearing a piece of cheesecake. He was part of this family of believers? It was that easy to belong?

He collected his own lunch and sat with Oliver. When they finished, they began cleanup.

"There are three full pies left in the carrier," Oliver told him. "Plus about eight pieces left on that table. What's your plan?"

"Leave them for anyone who wants them." Drew felt somewhat deflated now. "Unless you…?"

"Uh-uh. I've still got half the apple pie you gave me." Oliver smiled. "This was a good idea, Drew. Everyone loved it."

"Yeah." Drew shrugged. "Wish I'd thought of bringing along ice cream."

"Didn't need it. Those awesome pies were enough. Good job."

"Thanks." Drew wondered when this man had become such a good friend. "You, too, Ollie. Couldn't have managed without your help."

"I just hope Mandy doesn't cuff your ears when she realizes you raided Bonnie's garden for that rhubarb." Oliver guffawed at Drew's scowl. "Let's get cleanup finished so you can get going. Tell Bonnie and Ben hi from me?"

"Sure will."

It took them less than fifteen minutes thanks to a well-organized director who had done this many times before.

"Great idea to use paper plates for the pie." Pastor Joe applauded. "Makes cleanup easier. I think our moms really appreciated this lunch. Good work."

Drew emerged from the church feeling tired, but in a good way. Mandy and Ella were seated on the grass in a sunlit patch of grass, reading a book.

"Sorry to make you wait," he apologized.

"No problem, chef." Mandy's grin added an appealing glow to her tanned face. "That pie was amazing."

"Thanks." He tried to play it down, but she wouldn't let him.

"Truly, Drew. You went to a lot of trouble. I just have one question—"

"Yes," he said before she could ask. "Yes, I picked Bonnie's rhubarb. It needed it."

Mandy burst out laughing. She rose and tugged Ella upward, shoulders shaking.

"What's so funny?" he demanded.

"Your guilty face," she sputtered.

He rolled his eyes and waited until she sobered.

"Actually, I wasn't going to ask about the rhubarb. I was going to ask about your pie recipe."

"Oh. It's Bonnie's. She taught me to make pies many

years ago." He blinked. "I have the cake I made for her in the car, but maybe I should have brought along some pie, too."

"Already done." Mandy pointed to the foil-covered plate sitting nearby.

"Good. Thank you." He wondered why she was just standing there. "Are you about ready to go?"

"I would be if I could find my car." Mandy glanced around the almost empty lot. "I thought you parked—?"

"I don't want to go in Mama's car," Ella said in an unusually cranky voice. "It's too pokey."

Drew mentally winced at the hurt look that flickered across Mandy's face.

"The mechanics are going to make sure your mom's car gets fixed because this time she's going to leave it as long as necessary. This time she's going to use Bonnie's car until hers is working perfectly," he said firmly. "Right?" He glanced at Mandy, waiting for her nod. "Oliver brought the pies in Bonnie's vehicle. He left it for us and took yours to drop off at the garage where he picked up his truck. It was in for a tire rotation."

Mandy shook her head. "Drew, I'm not sure I can afford—"

"That's why you never left it very long, because of the mechanics fees." He grimaced. "The Double H is paying, Mandy. You use your vehicle for all kinds of work errands. It's only fair the ranch pays for some wear and tear. Besides," he added when it looked like she'd argue, "it won't do anyone any good if you're stranded on the road somewhere. It benefits the Double H to keep your car operating."

"But—"

"Can we go?" Ella interrupted.

"Lead the way, missy." Drew glanced at Mandy. "What's wrong with her?" he asked sotto voce.

"What's wrong is that I don't got a daddy," Ella snapped, hands on her hips. "I'll be the only kid at church on Father's Day who doesn't got one." She stomped her way to Bonnie's car, flung herself into her seat in the back and buckled her belt, but her face remained uncharacteristically frowning.

Talk about guilting someone.

Drew tried to brush it off as he drove toward the hospital, but it wasn't easy. This child constantly amazed, confused and astounded him. Her days were mostly always sunny and she spread joy wherever she went. People smiled back at her because they couldn't help it. Her happiness was contagious, much as Mandy's had been. Life with Ella would be an unforgettable experience.

This past week Drew had grown to love Ella's laugh when she beat him at Chutes and Ladders, or raced him on her pony, or sprayed bubbles all over him. Her malleable nature and her constant inquisitiveness forced him to provide answers that satisfied her curious mind. Her effusive affection was growing on him, too. Once or twice he allowed himself the sweet pleasure of holding her, of feeling her velvet lips pressing against his cheek.

Somehow with Ella, Drew experienced freedom to express emotions he'd always feared. She was so much like her mother that he often caught himself glancing at Mandy to see if she remembered doing the same things Ella did.

But Ella wasn't sunny today. Every time he glanced in his rearview mirror, her tearstained face reflected like a dart that pierced his heart. Twice he caught Mandy watching him with an expression that said something between *fess up* and *admit you're a failure*.

Neither one was an option. But that didn't stop Drew from pondering what would happen if he told Ella he was her father. The notion barely flicked in his brain before his mind screamed, *No!*

Ella wanted a permanent daddy. That meant being there whenever she needed him, doing whatever it took to care for and protect her. It meant responsibility, which rendered the very notion of fatherhood impossible for Drew. Besides, Mandy didn't want him in her world permanently. She'd made that very clear when she'd excluded him by not revealing that she was having a baby. And in the years since.

Drew had done some responsible things. He'd set up a fund for Ella with Mandy as administrator. It would take care of any needs Ella might have now and for her future education. He'd spoken to his lawyers to revise his will so everything would go to Mandy. He would stay as promised to help her keep the ranch going, ensuring she'd still have her job. What more could he do?

Yet none of it seemed enough. All Drew kept hearing was *failure*.

Oliver's comments echoed in his head.

You make your home by contributing, by giving and by sharing with people you care about. Maybe that's why you never felt comfortable here, because you didn't put anything of yourself into making the ranch your home.

Maybe if…

"Drew? We exit here." Mandy's quiet voice broke through his musings and cut off things that would have been a mistake to consider.

"I know." He signaled and took the turnoff to the hospital. There was no going back.

Face it, buddy, a voice inside him chided. *You burned your bridges with Mandy years ago because you were too scared to keep searching for her, too afraid you'd find her and too terrified she'd ask you to give up your dream.*

That was all true.

Just because Drew still hadn't figured out where he belonged didn't mean he belonged at Hanging Hearts Ranch, no matter what Miss Partridge kept hinting.

Chapter Ten

"I'd forgotten exactly how grueling Cragg's Peak is." Mandy leaned against a spruce tree to rest her wobbly legs. She sipped wearily from her water bottle. "I'm getting old."

"Those guys are older than us by a decade, yet the climb doesn't seem to bother them." Drew grimaced at the three men gathered on a promontory overlooking the picturesque valley, animatedly chattering about how best to share their view with the world. "They're not even breathing heavy," he complained. "Yet I'm huffing and puffing like a man three times my age. How do they do it?"

"Don't ask," she hissed. When Drew's eyes widened, she explained, "They'll tell you clean living and then go into a long list of their power drinks and boosters, what they eat and what their fitness routine is. You'll feel worse after you hear it," she assured him.

"Not possible," Drew said mournfully, sliding down the tree trunk to rest on the pine-needled ground. "I thought yesterday would kill me, but I feel even worse now."

"I know." Mandy rubbed her neck. "When I crawled into my sleeping bag at eleven last night and zoned out, they were still catching up with work on their phones.

When I woke up at five, they were dressed, shaven and had eaten."

"They also drank all the coffee," Drew complained bitterly. "I didn't even get to breathe in the aroma from an empty pot."

A rush of sympathy oozed inside her. He did look destroyed. And gut-wrenchingly handsome with his scruffy chin.

"There wasn't anything to breathe because they don't drink coffee." She rolled her eyes at him. "Get over your addiction, Drew," she teased, loving this easy banter between them. It had been so long. She blinked at a sound and groaned. "Here they come. Look lively, cowboy." Through sheer brute force, she rose and pasted a smile on her lips. "Had enough of the view, gentlemen?"

"Who could get enough of that?" Rob, the leader, waved a hand to encompass the valley. The others chimed in their agreement. "We thought we might take a dip in that river to refresh ourselves for the next leg. That okay with you?"

"Sure, but it's frigid," Mandy warned them. "Fresh from the mountain snow. Drew here used to jump in as soon as the ice was melted. Aren't you joining these guys today?" she asked him, tongue in cheek.

"Think I'll pass." Drew's expression promised he'd get even later. "I want to check in with Oliver, make sure things are okay with Bailey and my favorite trail riders."

"I admire a guy who takes his work seriously." Rob ushered his friends into a grove of trees to change into their swimsuits.

Sheer force of will kept Mandy upright and smiling, humming a merry tune as she busied herself checking her pack until a jubilant shout erupted. Seconds later splashes echoed through the valley as the men dove in. Then she relaxed.

"They're nuts," Drew murmured, staring at the group.

"I've met a lot of odd investment guys, but these three are way beyond odd."

"Is that why you interrupted me earlier when I was about to tell them what you do?" Mandy asked, then winced as she stepped on her sore foot the wrong way.

"What's wrong?" Instantly Drew was by her side, looking for injuries.

"Nothing. My ankle is aching, that's all." She rubbed the offending member, surprised by his attentiveness.

"Let me take a look at it while they're swimming." He waited a moment, then arched his brow. "You know it's better to assess the problem immediately, Manda Panda."

"You're not responsible for me," she said firmly.

"Ben's number one tenet—when in the back country, everyone is responsible for everyone else. So?" Drew crossed his arms over his chest and waited. Clearly he was not giving up.

"Oh for goodness' sake," she muttered and undid her hiking boot. "It's nothing."

"So why the big deal about showing me? I have seen your foot before." As if aware he'd just alluded to their past, Drew tucked his chin into his chest, knelt in front of her and pulled off her sock. Then he began probing her ankle with his fingertips. "Does that hurt?"

"No," Mandy said, refusing to wince. "I'm fine."

"It looks a bit swollen. You should have stuck it in that frigid water. Since you didn't…" Drew removed the first aid kit from his pack and selected an elastic bandage. "Let me wrap it. If nothing's wrong, it won't matter. If it is tender and you're just being tough, it will help."

"Anyone ever tell you you're bossy?" she muttered as he began winding the bandage around her instep, heel and ankle.

"You. About a million times." He continued winding, then used a safety pin to hold it in place. "They're getting out of the water now. You might want to put your boot back on."

"Thanks." Mandy sounded gruff even to her own ears, but that was because she couldn't suppress a well of longing for the return of his gentle touch. It had been so long since she'd felt cared for, cherished, protected—loved?

Love was not for her. Mandy pushed out the wayward thoughts and tied her laces. She'd just finished when the men reappeared looking hale and hearty.

"Good swim?" Drew asked from his seat atop a huge boulder.

"Fantastic!" The eldest of the men held up his phone. "But I'd appreciate it if we could take the quickest way back. I've got an emergency at work."

"That's too bad," Drew offered. He shot Mandy a sideways glance she couldn't interpret. "The shortest way back would be straight down, but we're not going to rappel today. There's been no appreciable rain for a while and a lot of rocks are loose and falling. We don't want to get hit on the head."

"No." Rob studied him curiously. "But there is a rough trail down and across the pasture, right?"

"Yes, there is, but we won't be going that way either." Drew smiled to soften his sharp response. "Bulls," he explained. "They're feeding in that area so it's better we avoid them. Shall we gear up? Don't worry, we'll get back in good time and we'll see some lovely flora and fauna along the way. You'll have great pictures."

Bulls? There were no bulls in that pasture. Mandy knew that for certain because she'd ridden out two days ago specifically to check the area they'd be traveling through. When Drew ignored her, grabbed his walking stick and moved to the head of the trail, she had no choice but to bring up the rear.

Which made her wonder what he was up to, because

by moving in as leader, Drew was taking responsibility for the rest of the trek, for their guests and for any misadventure that might happen along the way. Drew, the man who avoided responsibility like the plague.

There wasn't time to debate with him, and anyway they'd look like idiots arguing in front of their guests. At least he'd grabbed the food pack along with his own equipment, meaning she wouldn't have to carry it. That would significantly lighten her load. And since everyone was in front of her, no one would notice if she limped or favored her foot.

Drew wasn't stupid. He knew exactly what he was doing by taking the lead. The question was, why had he done it?

Drew knew Mandy didn't understand his actions, and he wasn't about to confirm that he knew her ankle wasn't one hundred percent or that she would suffer more if they took the return path she'd planned. She would be struggling by the end of the day anyway given the darkening bruise he'd seen on her leg. She must have fallen somewhere along the way. Why hadn't he noticed?

Because their guests were restless traveling this easy trail, he searched his brain for unusual things to point out to keep them interested.

"I'm sure you already know that Glacier was the first International Peace Park formed in 1932," Drew said. "Early management felt that the upper Glacier Valley shouldn't be divided between the US and Canada so the two parks joined together with both working to preserve the wilderness. Hence Waterton and Glacier National Parks meet on the countries' boundaries."

"Right. Bear grass is a mountain lily common to both parks." Mandy looked somewhat deflated when Rob gave a bored nod. "The long basal leaves were great for making watertight baskets by aboriginal people," she added.

These so-called environmentalists seemed to grow a little more interested.

"Why is there a fence around those ferns?" Rob asked.

"To protect them. Waterton moonwarts are considered the rarest moonwart in that park. Its appearance here is very unusual, so since it's growing on our land, we try to make sure it can multiply. We're very close to the park boundary here." Drew lurched to a stop. "Don't talk," he whispered. "Just watch."

Below them a massive grizzly was at the creek's edge, fishing with his paw. He seemed unperturbed by the click of the bankers' camera lenses as he studiously dipped into the water. Finally he snagged a fish and began tearing into it. The men appeared enthralled. When Mandy took a break on a grassy patch nearby, Drew felt a sense of satisfaction. He could do this.

And then Rob moved.

"No!" Drew ordered as loudly as he dared.

But the banker, intent on getting his picture, stepped forward, landed on some shale and immediately began sliding. The grizzly glanced up from his fish, spied Rob and lumbered to his feet. In a flash Drew had his noisemaker and bear spray in hand. If they didn't work...

Rob remained unmoving as the grizzly continued to stare at him.

"Don't move a muscle," Drew said in his softest voice. "They don't have great eyesight. It could be that he only heard the stones shift. Wait."

They waited, collectively holding their breath. Mandy noiselessly appeared at his side.

"We're going to have to retreat, go around him," she murmured, her warm breath brushing his face.

The bear seemed to hear her because he stretched tall again and began slowly moving toward them.

"Wait." Drew held up his hand in an agreed-upon signal that everyone should remain in place. "We're down-wind of him. He hasn't got our scent. He's just curious about the noise." He was certain his low-voiced comment did not reach the bear, who seemed suddenly sidetracked by a pretty fawn dashing through the clearing. "Give it a few minutes, Mandy."

She met his gaze steadfastly, held it, then finally nod-ded. "Okay," she said. "You're the boss."

Meaning he was responsible if something happened.

Feeling his throat choke up at the weight of that, Drew turned his head to retract his statement but she was gone, creeping back to her hiding place. Gulping down his fear, he mentally rehearsed the strategies Ben had taught him. If the bear charged, he was ready. If he hung around, they'd stay put—

The bear moved forward.

If ever there was a time to pray, Drew figured this was it. What was that verse John had quoted? *I will lift up mine eyes unto the hill from whence cometh my help. My help cometh from the Lord.* Meaning he didn't have to handle this himself, that God was there waiting to be asked?

I know I haven't followed You much, but we need Your help. Please? Drew prayed the words with his eyes wide open, hoping that assuming leadership wouldn't prove to be his biggest mistake.

"He's going." Rob's mutter drew sighs of relief from the others.

They all watched the bear move away. Stunned by this answer to his prayer, Drew used his binoculars to follow its progress until it disappeared into brush that was no-where near the path he planned to take. *Thank you, God.*

"Let me help you up," he said, thrusting out a hand to Rob. "I'm sorry you had to stay there for so long but—"

"Serves me right," the older man said. "I need to think

before acting. Something I've always struggled with, I'm afraid. But I sure got some good pictures."

"Are you okay? Nothing damaged?" Mandy asked.

"Only my pride." With a rueful countenance, he rejoined his friends and apologized for putting them at risk.

"At least he realizes his mistake," Mandy said almost under her breath as she joined Drew. "But I don't think we'll accept another trip from them."

"Because of a bear?" Drew agreed with her but wondered why she'd changed her mind.

"No. And the fee is great," she said softly. "But this trip has taken too much time from our usual activities and I now wonder if we'll receive as much good publicity as I'd hoped." She glanced over one shoulder, then made a face at Drew. "Rob's too interested in his pictures, not enough in the land and what it offers."

He let that pass. "Is your foot okay?"

"It's fine. Let's go."

But as they negotiated the rough terrain, Drew noticed that Mandy walked more slowly, then mincingly. And her happy smile grew more forced. She was not okay, and his concern for her grew the farther they went. When they stopped for a rest, he called Oliver, asked him to saddle some horses and meet them at a certain spot.

"Don't ask why," he ordered. "We'll be waiting."

When Drew ended the call, Mandy was at his elbow. "Trouble?"

"No. But Oliver's taking a group for a short ride tonight and I'm going along. So I asked him to meet us at Eagle's Corner with horses. That way we can get back a bit earlier and I'll have time to take a break before we leave."

"You don't have to go, Drew. Someone else can do that," she said with a frown.

"Actually they can't. Lanny wanted the evening off for a special date with his wife. I said I'd cover for him."

In fact, Drew had told the young hand he'd cover for him *if* he was back in time, but Mandy didn't need to know that. Besides, he wanted her off that foot, fast.

"It will be fine," he assured her.

Drew explained his plan to the men. Noticing Mandy's barely concealed limp, he added that he'd like a few more minutes to soak in the view before they resumed the hike. He pretended to take a bunch of pictures with his phone, giving the impression that they might be for a publicity campaign for Ben. But he couldn't stall very long. The men were eager to return.

Oliver met them before they reached Eagle's Corner. The bankers were knowledgeable riders and it took only a short time for the group to arrive back at the ranch. Though Mandy gallantly leaned against a fence post while bidding the men goodbye, Drew could see she was hurting. He barely waited until the expensive SUV had driven off the ranch before scooping her into his arms.

"What are you doing?" she demanded, eyes stretched wide in shock.

"Getting you off that foot. Which you injured. Didn't you?" Drew caught Oliver watching them with a huge grin spread across his face. "Can you handle the horses?"

"No problem, buddy." The older man's mocking smile didn't diminish one whit as he led the horses away.

"Well?" Drew strode across the yard, Mandy in his arms, aware yet uncaring that half the staff watched. "What happened?"

"I fell." She glared at him as he climbed the stairs to her front door. "It's no biggie. Just a sprain."

"A sprain so bad it hurts you to walk. Yes, that's *all*." He walked inside and set her on the sofa, arranged pillows at her back and then began undoing her boot, suddenly unreasonably angry that she'd tried to hide the injury from him.

"I can—"

"Sit there and do as you're told," Drew ordered irritably, but he used the utmost caution as he took off her boot and sock. The extent of the swelling made him suck in his breath. The bruise had more than tripled in size and was now a dark and angry black-blue. He gently propped her leg on a cushion. "I'll get some ice."

In the kitchen he found no ice in the freezer, but there was a bag of frozen peas. He grabbed it and some towels and returned to the sofa where Mandy lay with her eyes closed. Gingerly, fearing he'd add to her pain, he placed a towel over her foot, then laid the bag of peas on top.

"When did it happen?" he demanded.

"I tripped yesterday," she began, then stopped when he hissed his breath between clenched teeth. She looked at him innocently. "You're overreacting," she said quietly. "I'm fine."

"You will be," he assured her, still furious, mostly because she'd been suffering for so long and had kept it from him. "As long as you stay on that couch and let the swelling go down."

"But I have to—" She stopped, frowned at his shaking head. "Really, Drew, I must do—"

"Nothing, Mandy," he finished. "Go nowhere. You're going to stay put and I'm going to make sure you do. I need to take a shower, but I'll be back to make dinner. When I get back, you'd better be lying right where I left you," he ordered.

Her eyes widened at his tone but she said nothing.

Drew had a thousand other things he wanted to add, about how she was always making sure everyone else had what they needed and now it was time for the favors to be reciprocated, but he was lousy at words and in no mind to put them together properly right now.

"I'll be back," he promised and then left her house. On his way to Bonnie and Ben's place, he called the doctor the ranch had on retainer and asked him to come and check Mandy over. He also called Lanny and apologized but insisted he simply could not fill in for him tonight.

By the time Drew had showered, grabbed some fresh vegetables from Bonnie's garden and selected two steaks from the freezer, the doctor's car was sitting in front of Mandy's. He walked in the door just in time to hear the medical verdict.

"It's sprained, Mandy. Badly," Doc Malfort said. "The only thing you can do is rest until it's better. I'm guessing that will take the best part of a week."

"A week?" Mandy stared at him in disbelief. "I don't have a week to lie around."

"My dear, you don't have an option." The elderly man patted her hand consolingly. "When it comes to recuperation, you either take the time your body needs to heal now, or you push it and take much longer later because you've aggravated the injury. My advice is to do it now."

"My advice, too, Doc," Drew agreed as he set his groceries on the countertop.

"Smart man." Doc offered one of his rare smiles, then turned back to Mandy. "I'm not giving you pain pills. I know you, Mandy. If something dulls the pain, you'll push through and do too much. Rest. It won't be unbearable."

"It will for me," she grumbled. "But thanks for coming out."

"I was heading this way anyway." Doc glanced at Drew. "You have the information I want?"

"Yes, sir. Let's step outside and discuss it." Ignoring Mandy's curious frown, he escorted the doctor outside, away from the house, spent a few moments revealing his research on the company Doc had asked about, then returned inside.

Mandy sat with her arms crossed over her chest. "What information?"

"A fund he wants to invest in for his grandkids." Drew began assembling dinner, seasoning the steak and then cleaning the vegetables from the garden.

"You do fund investment now?" she asked curiously.

"I research whatever people want to know. Besides, it gave me a chance to do in-depth research for a new contract I might take on." He wrapped foil around the potatoes, assembled the salad and then realized he didn't know if she had a barbecue.

"On the back deck," Mandy said, reading his glance out the front window.

When he returned from starting the grill, Mandy glared at him.

"What's wrong?"

"You've been here a while now, Drew," she snapped. "Don't you have any inner longing to take over from your parents and run Hanging Hearts?"

"Why?" he said with a cocky grin. "Are you retiring?"

"I'm serious. Isn't there some yen buried inside you to come back to this gorgeous land? Doesn't this place have any hold on you at all?"

Drew knew from her tone that she was dead serious. He figured it was about time he was honest. He owed her that. He sat in the chair across from her, trying to put it together mentally in a way she'd understand. Finally he gave up and just spoke from his heart.

"I like being back," he said quietly. "I love getting up in the morning and smelling that scent of horses and mountain flowers—freshness, I guess you'd call it. I like being able to ride whenever I want—mostly," he added and shot her a crooked grin. "I'm even starting to enjoy the visitors who come here."

"I knew you'd come around," she said smugly.

"But I like my other work, too. I love the challenge of figuring out how to collate tons of data so I can see a pattern in what a stock or market has done and the probabilities that it will go in the direction I think." Drew smiled at the thought of his newest and most challenging project yet. "I love the research of mentally traveling all over the world, forming a hypothesis and then watching to see if I was close or way off."

"You love New York." She sounded disappointed.

"Who doesn't love New York?" He shrugged. "But it's not the city that keeps me there. It's accessibility to the markets."

"Yet you've been doing your work from here." She sounded puzzled.

"Yes." Drew nodded. "I wasn't sure how that would work, but it's turning out very well."

"Except you're working all night," she pointed out.

"Not all night and not every night. Anyway, people all over the world have shiftwork and they don't die from it. Sometimes I get my best ideas in the silence of the night." Drew heard something unspoken in her voice. "What's really bothering you, Mandy?"

"It's just—I thought maybe once you were here, you'd realize—" She stopped abruptly and shook her head. "Never mind. The grill's probably ready."

"Yeah." Drew carried out the food, set it carefully on the grates, then adjusted the heat while reviewing what she'd said. Confusion filled him. Mandy had hoped he'd change his mind? Why?

He returned deep in thought, trying to figure out a way to tell her the truth.

"Can we sit outside? It's such a gorgeous night." She'd already risen from the sofa, a crutch the doctor had left tucked under one arm.

Drew followed behind her in case she lost her footing or her balance. While she got comfortable on the rattan love seat, he concentrated on the steaks and setting the small table. It didn't take long before everything was ready. They ate in silence, the sound of crickets and frogs filling the evening air. Though Drew would have devoured the meal at any other time, tonight he just couldn't summon an appetite.

"I miss Ella," he admitted.

"Me, too, but I know she's loving camp." Mandy looked at him. "It's delicious but I don't think I can eat any more, Drew."

"Me neither." He carried the dirty dishes inside, put them in the sink and stored the leftovers. With the kitchen clean, there was no more putting off the inevitable. He prepared a pitcher of Mandy's favorite iced tea with lemon, then carried two glasses of it outside while mentally voicing a second prayer for help. Drew felt no immediate response, but then remembered that John had said God didn't always answer on demand.

"Mandy." Once she'd tasted her tea and approved, Drew took his seat across from her. He drew her hands in his and met her gaze head on. "We need to talk." She inclined her head and he pushed on. "You've been hoping that once I came back I'd realize how much I missed this place and decide to live here permanently. Right?" He could see the truth in her eyes. "I can't. I'm sorry."

She pulled her hands away from his but never broke his stare. "Why not?"

"Because."

"Because of me?" she demanded. "Ella?"

"Yes, to both. And a thousand other reasons. Wait!" he said when she looked about to interrupt. "Let me say this, Mandy."

She leaned back, folded her hands in her lap and studied him.

"All those years ago—I did love you, Mandy. Maybe in some way I still do but..." He cut off that revealing train of thought and forced himself to focus. "Back then I thought we'd get married. It's probably a good thing that didn't happen."

"Because?"

Drew saw the way her face closed up, hiding her true feelings. He needed to say this. He owed her that much.

"I—uh—"

"I'm a captive audience, Drew," she said sharply, a trace of gritty determination glinting from her emerald eyes. "Please, go on."

Drew took a deep breath and plunged into his confession, hoping desperately that when he finished, Mandy wouldn't hate him.

Chapter Eleven

"I'm not good at responsibility," Drew began.

Mandy opened her mouth, ready to refute that. He didn't give her the chance.

"How many times have you had to send Oliver to find me because I forgot a class?"

"You work late," she excused, but Drew shook his head.

"I took on the job here knowing what was required." His tone softened. "You have a child to care for, Mandy, and an entire ranch. You're up in the wee hours of the morning tending to stock or foals or equipment problems and you still manage to get to work on time. I imagine that holds true if Ella has a bad night, too."

"Whatever." She wasn't going to argue about it. Not now. If she could just forget those words of his—*I loved you. Maybe I still do*—if she could get Drew to finish and leave her alone, she could finally give way to the pain and despair boiling inside. "Go on."

"I can't be Ella's father. Ever."

His words hit her like a freight truck. Mandy struggled to hide how decimated she felt.

"I'm sorry if that's what you hoped. I'm not shirking my responsibilities. I've set up a fund for her," he said, his voice brisk, businesslike. "You are administrator of that fund and you can access it whenever you wish. I've made sure that if Ella ever needs anything, the money will be there."

"But *you* won't be." Fury lit a fuse in her heart but Mandy would not, could not give in to it because it wouldn't help. "Ella doesn't want or need your money, Drew. Or things that it can buy. She wants a father to love her and share her life."

"I know. But that can't be me." There was no give in his adamant response. "She's a great kid and I care about her far more than I ever knew I could. I want Ella to be healthy and successful, to reach every goal she strives for."

"You just don't want to be there for it," Mandy said coolly.

"I can't."

"Because you're not responsible," she prodded.

Drew nodded but said nothing, because there was nothing more to say. And still Mandy refused to give up. For Ella's sake, she told herself.

"Wasn't it responsible to get me back here once you realized I'd hurt my ankle?" she asked. "Wasn't it responsible to take those bankers on their trip so there would be money for your parents' renovations? To keep them interested with your stories, to make sure they understood the risks of everything they wanted to try?"

"You did that, not me."

"Me?" Mandy smiled and shook her head. "I'm not the one who decided which trail we should come back on or arranged it so I'd bring up the rear, which allowed me to pause without anyone noticing. I'm not the one who called Oliver to bring horses or offered to take over for Lanny when there was no one else."

"I canceled that. Anyway, that was—"

"Responsibility," she interrupted. "I'm not the one who reorganized Ben's entire accounting system and discovered we'd been overcharged by one of our suppliers." She smiled at his surprise. "Yes, I know what you've been up to. That's you, Drew. You being responsible."

He shook his head, but his eyes remained on her. That gave her courage to continue, to try to help him see who he really was.

"What do you think responsibility is about?" She smiled at his blink of confusion. "You harp on your lack of responsibility so much that I looked it up. One of the definitions is being able to answer for one's conduct and obligations. As in trustworthy." Mandy reached out and touched his cheek, unable to stop herself and needing that small comfort. "You are trustworthy, Drew. What you've just told me about this fund for Ella proves it."

He shook his head. "That's only doing the right thing," he muttered.

"Another definition of responsibility is knowing right from wrong. God gave you tons of responsibility, Drew. All you have to do is trust Him to show you how to use it."

Mandy could see that he wasn't able to accept this, couldn't get past his preconceptions. She wouldn't prolong the conversation, not tonight when she was hurting and too vulnerable. Eager to escape before she begged him to be part of her world again permanently, Mandy rose without thinking. She yelped as pain shot up her leg.

Before she could blink, Drew had swung her into his arms and carried her into the house. He set her on the sofa, then went to fetch her crutch and their used glasses. He placed his empty one in the sink but refilled hers and set it on the table by the sofa where she could reach it.

"You need to rest now," he said firmly, his fingertips brushing her jawline. Was that a hint of anger tingeing the cracks in his voice? "Can you manage to get to bed or should I call Trina?"

"I'm fine. I can manage just fine," she insisted, trying

not to lean into his touch. Drew didn't look convinced so she added, "Leave Trina alone. She has a big date with a guy she likes. I'm not going to spoil that."

Drew studied her for a few more moments. Finally he nodded. "You have your phone?"

She pointed to the table where it sat.

"Okay. I'll go. But if you need anything," he said harshly and repeated, "anything. You are to call me. Don't be a hero."

"No," she agreed, not quite able to smother a tiny grin. "We have quite enough heroes around here today."

Drew rolled his eyes and gave her a disgusted look before heading toward the door. He paused there for a moment, then turned around and threw her a quirky smile.

"I guess this means you won't be making coffee tomorrow morning, Manda Panda. Too bad. Good night." After a long-suffering sigh, he left, the door softly closing behind him.

"Thank you," she called, but it was too late. He was gone.

"Get used to it," she told herself. "He'll soon be gone for good."

Mandy let herself think about Drew, the way he'd cared for her, made sure the doctor visited and then foraged for a meal that would make chefs drool. Imagining him tiptoeing into Bonnie's sacrosanct garden to pick lettuce, a green onion and dill for the salad make her chuckle out loud. He'd even made her favorite iced tea without being asked.

Responsible? Drew went above and beyond responsibility.

She loved that about him. Because she loved him. Her heart had never found anyone else but Drew. He *was* Ella's father, like her in so many ways, if he would only see that.

But Drew wasn't staying. He didn't love her.

Tears welled as Mandy accepted reality. He wasn't going

to reconsider or see the error of his ways or go through some enlightenment that would suddenly reveal a gritty determination to be the father her little girl so longed for, or the man who held her heart. And it didn't do her or Ella any good to keep hoping, pretending or wishing it would ever be otherwise.

Mandy let her tears flow while her hopes and dreams died. But tears didn't help.

So as the moon slid out from beneath the clouds and lit the ranch yard, as the working sounds of the ranch died away and only a faint whinny of horses carried to the house, Mandy prayed for acceptance of God's will. It was the only way she knew to deal with her hurt.

By morning's dawning light she was able to accept that God wanted her to remain single. Hadn't she known since Ella's birth that romance and love were not for her? She'd ruined her chance at that.

She'd done without Drew's love this far. Though it hurt, she would continue to do so. She would put on her best face and do her job, maybe not the same as she'd done before her injury, but there were several calls she'd put off, business that could be done over the phone. Organizing the renovations for Bonnie and Ben's house now that they had funds for it was one. No one would notice that anything about her had changed.

Calf branding might have to wait, but as soon as Mandy could put a little weight on her foot, she'd ask one of the men to bring over a quad. She'd take it to the office and finish working on her spreadsheets so everything would be organized when her bosses returned. There were a thousand things to concentrate on. And when she ran out of them, she'd go online and order some new jeans. Hers were shabby and nothing about them gave off the aura of boss.

She was *not* going to admit that she wanted to look better while Drew was here.

Mandy would not mourn him. Not in public anyway. God had things for her to do. He'd been with her all these years, since the very darkest days after Ella's birth. She wouldn't look back. She would look ahead and wait to see what He had in store for her future.

Thus resolved, Mandy glanced around for her crutch. Her gaze snagged on the album on the lower shelf of the coffee table. Her "don't miss the beautiful things" album. The perfect reminder that God was faithful.

Tenderly she picked it up and opened the first page. Her sweet baby. Resolutely she pushed away every memory from that most difficult time except the wonder of her tiny daughter, every finger, every toe so perfectly formed by God himself. God had known what He was doing then and He knew now. Page after page, Mandy found answers to prayer in Ella's history.

"'They that wait upon the Lord shall renew their strength,'" she quoted. "Teach me, Lord, to wait."

Oh, Drew, her heart wept. *If you could only let go of your fear long enough to see the wonder of our precious child.*

At last she fell asleep.

Drew set his phone alarm for five thirty in the morning even though he hadn't finished his own work until well after one. Responsibility was earned. It was about time he stopped taking and started giving. Was that God's prompt inside his head? He wasn't sure. He only knew it was time he helped Mandy.

This wasn't about love, he told himself. It was about being a friend to someone who had repeatedly been there for him. Allowing love into it wasn't possible because he wasn't staying and he couldn't pretend otherwise.

By six, Drew was holding a quick staff meeting to explain that Mandy was nursing a severe ankle sprain and would not be available. The staff was to come to him with all questions and problems. Oliver helped him figure out the most pressing issues and organize the hands to deal with them. Thankfully Drew was not scheduled to escort a group today so he spent a couple of hours studying Mandy's notes in her office and checking her calendar. The sight of the dormant computer reminded him that he hadn't kept his promise to finish her spreadsheet program. He grabbed the little notebook out of his shirt pocket and added that to his growing to-do list.

At the sound of a car motor, Drew stepped outside and saw Trina driving through the gate. He walked over and explained the situation.

"Maybe Mandy won't want me fussing over her this early," Trina said. "I could work at my place for a while on some stuff for Ella's birthday on Saturday."

Drew had completely forgotten about that. He'd only intended to stay six weeks, which would end on Saturday, but how could he walk away on Ella's big day, while Mandy was incapacitated?

"Drew?"

"Oh, sorry. Thinking." He quickly nodded. "Go ahead, Trina. Mandy's probably still sleeping anyway. I'll check on her in a bit, see if she needs anything."

"She had some things she wanted me to do in the house while Ella's at camp. You're sure it's okay if I leave now?" Trina didn't look convinced that Drew could handle whatever Mandy needed.

"I'm sure," he said firmly. "Go."

"Okay. Back in a couple of hours." Trina drove away.

It was almost eight o'clock by the time Drew found a moment to check on Mandy. He tapped gently on the door before stepping inside, not wanting to disturb her. To his dismay, she lay on the sofa, exactly where he'd left her the night before, wearing the same clothes. She was clutching a book to her chest, and when he pried it from her, she woke up.

"Oh," she said, blinking the sleep from her beautiful green eyes. "Hi. I just dozed off."

"Uh-huh." He showed her his watch and laughed at her gasp of disbelief, amused by the way she shoved long, wayward strands of blond hair out of her eyes. "How's the foot?"

He asked it just as she shifted her leg to the floor and made to stand. She shrieked and flopped back against the cushions, hissing her breath between her teeth like an angry snake.

"Does that answer your question?" she gasped.

"Pretty much." Drew studied the book he held. Don't Miss The Beautiful Things. Probably very personal. He stifled his urge to peek inside by setting it on the coffee table. What exactly were the beautiful things?

"Man, that hurts. I forgot—oh, ouch!" She eased her leg onto the cushions. "I really need a cup of coffee." She handed him the melted bag of peas with a mournful face.

"You're not the only one," Drew muttered.

"Well—" Mandy studied him. "If I tell you step by step, can you try to make some? Please? I'm desperate."

"I know the feeling, but you know that my coffee never turns out." He wasn't going to try again and fail again. Well, he wasn't until he really looked at Mandy and saw pain filling her lovely eyes. With a sigh of surrender, he walked to her kitchen. "What's first? Water, right?" He turned on the tap.

"No, not that water," she said. "It's too hard. Take it from the water cooler."

"Maybe that's why my coffee's never good," he said thoughtfully.

"Drew, come on," Mandy urged. "Withdrawal is about to set in. Fill the pot with that water. The coffee is in the fridge, in a canister. See it?" she asked as he peered into the fridge.

"Okay, but why is it in the fridge?" he asked with a frown.

"I'm not sure, but that's how I learned to make it for my dad so that's how I've kept doing it. Have you got a clean filter in the basket? Good. You need to find a yellow plastic spoon in the drawer."

Drew held up a tablespoon. "Will this do?"

"Yellow. Plastic." Mandy sighed as if her patience was running thin. She must need coffee worse than he did.

"It's not here—wait." He spied a weird shaped yellow spoon at the back of the drawer and dragged it out. "This thing?"

"Yes. Now measure exactly three spoons of coffee into the basket. No!" she squealed before he could dump even one. "Too much. Just a level spoonful."

"Who knew it was an exact science?" he muttered to himself, following her directions precisely with exaggerated movements. "Or that you're so bossy?"

"I heard that," she said with a glower. "Okay, put the basket in place, dump the water in and place the pot underneath. It will start dripping immediately."

Not quite sure it was as easy as that, Drew stood watching. Within seconds the fragrant aroma of fresh brewed coffee hit his nostrils.

"It worked," he chortled. "I think I actually made good coffee."

"We'll have to taste it to know for sure," Mandy warned. "It will take about three minutes to brew. Can we talk while that's happening?"

"Sure." Drew walked to the chair he'd sat in last night and folded himself into it. "What's up?"

"Business. There are a couple of things that must be

done today." Mandy blinked when he pulled his notebook from his pocket. "What's that?"

"To-do list." He licked his pencil, ready to write. "Shoot." When Mandy didn't speak, he glanced up, found her gaping at him.

"Did you just say *shoot*?" she asked in disbelief.

"Yeah. So?" Drew didn't get whatever was going on in her mind, but then he'd never been great at reading people.

"Who are you and what have you done with Drew Calhoun?" Mandy burst out laughing at his surprise. "*Shoot*? What are you, some kind of Hollywood cowboy?"

She chortled so long and so hard that Drew returned his pencil and notebook to his pocket and went to find out if the coffee was as good as it smelled. It was.

"I make good coffee," he said smugly after taking a sip. "Extremely good."

"So share already, cowboy." Mandy scrutinized his every move as he poured coffee into her mug and then added cream. "It smells amazing." She accepted the cup from him and inhaled. "I wish I'd had a cup of this about two hours ago."

She did everything with such full-bodied zest, even enjoying her morning coffee. First she tasted it, just a drop or two on her tongue. Then she took a bigger sip. Drew suddenly realized he was staring. He gulped his last mouthful, clamped on his hat and headed to the door.

"Okay, tell me what *must* be done first so I can get to work," he said. "Trina's working on some birthday stuff for Ella but she'll be back shortly. You good till then?"

"Yes. After I have a second or perhaps third cup of coffee, I'm having a shower." Mandy held up her hand to stop him. "Don't say it!" she ordered. "I'll agree to wait till Trina gets back, but I am having a shower." She told him the immediate issues that needed handling, then added, "Don't mess up my ranch, Drew!"

"Shades of Miss Partridge," he muttered with a John Wayne imitation tip of his hat. After setting the thermal carafe of coffee and the cream pitcher on the table near her, he left, humming a tune.

"Funny how a little coffee cheers you up," Oliver teased when he caught up to Drew a few minutes later. "Or is it the company you keep?"

"Oh, get over yourself." Drew tugged a sheet of paper from his back pocket and unfolded it. "While Mandy's laid up, she wants these things done. I want to add some to-do's of my own. Having worked here for a while, I have some ideas of how this place could run a little easier for Bonnie, Ben and Mandy. Want to help me?"

"Would these be the same ideas the boss nixed when you first came because she said they were too expensive?" Oliver studied the sheet of paper, then frowned at Drew.

"They're not that expensive," he countered. "Anyway, I'm paying for the supplies. It will be my Mother and Father's Day gifts." He grinned at Oliver's skeptical face. "In or not?

"Anything that helps Mandy, Bonnie and Ben is something I want to be part of. What's first?" Oliver scratched his head as he studied the number of entries.

"The gate. It's too narrow and too low for the big trucks to get in, which makes it really tedious to load stock for market. Anyway, I don't think our guests want to watch that when they're here for a riding lesson or a trek. Come on. I'll show you my plan."

"The boss is going to be, uh, gobsmacked." Oliver guffawed at Drew's glower.

Mandy *would* be surprised, but she'd also be happy about this new loading method because it would take less time and effort for everyone and probably reduce the stress on the herd. When it came to Hanging Hearts Ranch, Mandy was all about efficiency.

Drew received a couple of texts about two new contracts for his own business. He accepted the simplest one but declined the other because it would take too long. He wanted to be relatively free to continue running the Double H for as long as Mandy needed to heal. He'd already planned to shorten his working hours at night to a fraction of his usual six-hour day. When he got back to New York, he'd be able to work whenever and for as long he wanted. Sadly, there'd be nothing and no one there to distract him.

It struck Drew then that leaving the ranch was not going to be as simple as he'd thought when he first agreed to come. He hated that he'd be going without finishing everything he'd begun, but worse, that he'd be leaving Mandy and Ella vulnerable because no one would be here to watch out for them until Ben was back on his feet.

Also, Drew was now a father and Mandy's temporary stand-in.

Nothing about his life was simple anymore.

On Friday afternoon Mandy sat in the car, waiting impatiently for Ella, watching other parents picking up their kids and listening to exciting tales about the five days they'd spent at Camp Tapawingo. Despite her painful foot, she'd flatly refused to stay home and wait for Drew to return with Ella. She needed to be here, to hug her daughter and make sure she was all right.

But what was taking Drew so long?

"Stupid foot," she muttered, glaring at her bandaged ankle.

"Mama!" Ella raced toward her, dark ringlets flying in the breeze, eyes glowing and that big, generous smile wreathing her face.

"Hi, sweetie." Mandy pushed her car door open and half turned, arms ready to hug her precious child. "You look so much bigger," she said after receiving a tight squeeze and a big kiss. "You must have grown two inches."

"I still fit my clothes." Puzzled, Ella pulled at her T-shirt. "If I was bigger, it wouldn't fit—oh!" Her eyes grew as she caught sight of the support bandage around Mandy's ankle. "Did you get hurt, Mama?"

"I did hurt my foot, but it's getting better every—"

Ella whirled around to face Drew, glaring at him. "You din't keep your promise. You said you'd look after Mama good an' you din't," she said angrily. "You lied."

Although startled by Ella's outburst, Mandy was more shocked by Drew's response. He didn't argue, didn't tell Ella that he had tried. He didn't make excuses for himself. He simply stood there and let Ella berate him. When she was finished, he nodded.

"I didn't do enough to look after your mama and I'm very sorry, Ella."

"No, wait. Ella, honey, this wasn't Drew's fault. I tripped—"

"He promised. A promise is a promise," Ella insisted, chin thrust out.

"Yes, it is. And I broke my promise," Drew admitted. "But I'm doing my very best to make up for it, Bella Ella. I even learned how to make coffee for your mom."

Mandy rolled her eyes. He *would* say making coffee was his most important skill.

"Will you forgive me, Ella?" he asked, squatting in front of her.

"Yup. I hafta." She nodded. "God forgived me, so I hafta forgive you. That's what we learned here." She leaned forward and hugged him. Then she said in a not-quite-whisper, "You can buy me a nice present to make up. It's my birthday tomorrow."

"Ella!" Mandy tried to remonstrate her child, but Drew's shout of laughter drowned her out. "Stop it," she ordered, but he couldn't and soon neither could she. All the same, once Ella was fastened into her seat, Mandy said, "You and I need to have another talk about manners, my girl."

"No, Mama. I was jus' teasing Drew. He knowed it." She grinned at the man in question before adding in an earnest tone, "But it really is my birthday tomorrow. Did Trina make me a cake?"

"No, I'm doing that."

"You?" Mandy blinked at Drew.

"Yes, me. Why not? I made pies. I made a cake for Bonnie. Don't you think I can bake Ella a cake as good as Trina's?" He looked positively smug. But then, Mandy admitted, Drew had looked that way the entire week, as if he'd never had more fun in his life.

That worried her a little.

"The one you made for Bonnie was delicious, so I'm sure that you, the master coffee maker who arrives every morning at 7:00 a.m. To prove his skill, can absolutely bake and decorate a child's birthday cake," she said, tongue in cheek. "That you want to is—um, unexpected. What are you making? A castle? Last year Ella had a ladybug cake. The year before it was—" She tried to remember. "Ella, what was it?"

"I don't 'member," the little girl said. "We gotta look in the beautiful things book, I guess."

"Well, whatever Bella Ella wants, I will try to create." Drew chuckled at Mandy's dubious expression until Ella launched into a description of everything she'd done at camp, filling the drive home with her tales.

Mandy was content to let her talk. She didn't want to make conversation with Drew. Not that they didn't always find a lot to talk about, but she always kept it ranch-focused. Despite that, she still had to remind herself to stop noticing the way his longish hair curled at the edges of his Stetson, or the loping way he walked in his cowboy boots with just a hint of a swagger, or the sweet sound of his laughter that rang out more and more frequently. It was getting difficult to fight her feelings for him, especially when he seemed so excited to share work on the ranch.

This Drew was more like the man she'd known seven years ago, full of scenarios and possibilities, only this time they were all about the Double H. He stopped short of releasing actual details, but she knew his schemes were well-thought-out because there was always a scrunched-up paper peeking out of his back pocket and he consulted it frequently.

Then on Thursday evening, instead of leaving the ranch for his men's Bible study, the men had shown up at the ranch and disappeared into Ben and Bonnie's house. Why, Mandy wasn't exactly sure, but whatever it was ended up in a wiener roast around the fire pit in the back.

She found out more this morning when she got Trina to sneak her over to the main house in one of Ben's quads. The entire interior had been repainted and freshened up, completely erasing the damaged walls and trim the renovations had left.

How was she supposed to stop falling in love with a man who did that for his parents? Just listening to him now with Ella, Drew was tender, compassionate and gentle beyond words. Mandy was content to listen unabashedly to his voice and see his smile. Ella clearly bloomed in his presence.

The thing Mandy had to force herself to accept was that Drew wasn't staying. She'd heard him promise someone over the phone that once he was back in New York, they'd meet. She figured he was only waiting to leave until she was back on her feet.

"My driving is so good, your mama must have fallen asleep," Drew whispered to Ella.

"Maybe her foot hurts?" she whispered back.

"No, my foot doesn't hurt. And I'm not asleep. Just thinking about your birthday, sweetie." Mandy twisted to smile at her daughter. "Six. I can hardly believe it."

"An' the day after it is Father's Day." The joy drained from Ella's voice. "I prayed so hard to have a daddy for my birthday. How come God doesn't give me one?"

Mandy scrounged for an answer, but before she found one Drew spoke.

"I'm learning that God has His own time to do things, Ella. Time isn't the same for God as it is for us. He sees what we need and He knows when it's best to give it and when it's best for us to wait." His brow furrowed as he worked through his thought. "As you get older, Bella Ella, you'll have lots of times when you don't understand why God does or doesn't do something. That's when you have to remember His promises."

"What promises?" Ella leaned forward, eager to hear.

"Well, like this one. 'Be strong and of good courage, fear not, nor be afraid of them. For the Lord thy God, He it is that doth go with thee. He will not fail thee, nor forsake thee.' That's from Deuteronomy."

"I learned one in camp kinda like that. It was…" Ella scrunched up her face as she recalled the verse. "It said to trust God and not think I know it all. An' the second part was about asking God what to do when you don't know. It said He'll show you." She shrugged. "Sumthin' like that. The words get mixed up."

"That's in Proverbs. Good for you, Bella Ella," Drew encouraged. "Those are very good verses to know."

He sounded like a dad, acted like a dad. Why couldn't he just *be* Ella's dad?

He'll never be that when he learns your secret.

"I like camp," Ella said enthusiastically as they drove under the big metal sign welcoming them to Hanging Hearts Ranch. "But I like home better."

"Welcome home, Ella." Drew opened her door with a flourish and bowed at the waist.

Home. How much longer did she and her daughter have here, Mandy wondered? How much longer until Drew figured out that he truly belonged here?

How much time did she have before he demanded the truth and then told her to leave?

Chapter Twelve

Little girls' birthday parties were as foreign to Drew as being a daddy, but he was enjoying preparing for Ella's.

He and Trina had spent the morning blowing up balloons and hanging them all around the yard. He'd asked two hands to bring a picnic table and benches from one of the trail ride spots. They'd set them up in front of Mandy's house for the celebration.

Drew had rented a bouncy castle, hoping that six-year-old girls liked that kind of thing. There were water blasters to play with, a piñata to burst and a host of other activities Trina assured him would be fun for Ella and her friends. Hopefully Trina was right because this would probably be the only birthday of Ella's that Drew would attend, and he wanted everything perfect.

"You've really gone all out," Mandy said when he joined her on the deck for a cup of coffee. "Thank you for doing this. Ella's ecstatic."

"She's sure enjoying your gift." He chuckled as Ella wobbled around the yard, struggling to master the bicycle Mandy had given her.

Their daughter. That still amazed him.

"I don't think I ever properly thanked you for dropping

everything to come and help us out," Mandy said, meeting his gaze with her own but quickly breaking eye contact. "I appreciate it, Drew. Truly."

"I appreciate all you do for Ben and Bonnie. Including the house renovations," he added. "It's shocking what a difference those few changes you ordered have made. Pulling out that carpet and old flooring and replacing it with one level of hard floor will make moving around their place so much easier. New countertops that are smooth and unbroken, cabinet doors they only need to touch to open and will close themselves..." He shook his head. "Bonnie's never going to come out of her kitchen."

"I hope that's not true," Mandy teased.

"Except maybe to use that stunning bathroom." He looked at her seriously. "But that one excursion we took the bankers on couldn't possibly have paid for all those changes."

"Actually, the changes aren't quite complete, and no, their fee didn't cover everything," she said. "Turns out your parents' insurance policy has a clause in it that covers renovations when accessibility is an issue. The banker's money allowed us to get better quality finishes and complete the list the rehabilitation expert suggested. The painting you and your friends did really enhances all the changes."

"Aha, you've been wandering when you should be resting," he said.

"Trina took me. What?" she complained. "I was curious."

"And you wanted to make sure everything was just right." Drew nodded. "You take extremely good care of Ben and Bonnie. We three brothers haven't done as much as we should have for them," he admitted quietly. "It makes me ashamed."

"Your parents have been very good to me. I owe them."

Mandy frowned at him. "Why should you feel ashamed? I'm here, on site, all the time. It's easy for me to see the issues they have."

"Exactly. If we came more often, we would have noticed, too." Drew thrust his booted feet in front of him to stretch his long legs and glanced at her. "If you had unlimited funds, what else would you change for them?"

"New gutters," she said immediately. "If it ever rains again, their house needs better capability to get the water away from that old foundation. It's going to cause problems in another few years."

He studied the house critically.

"Downspouts would have to be extended. It's probably a good idea to use larger gutters, too. Okay, what else?" Drew's gaze shifted to Ella while his brain began organizing. "Might be an idea to get a new coat on the foundation, too."

"I like how you take an issue and think through all the angles that most people wouldn't even consider until much later," she murmured.

She liked the way he thought? He told himself not to read anything into that.

"What else?" he prodded to get the discussion off of him.

"I'd screen in their porch. Ben loves to sit out there in the evening, winter and summer. Bonnie, too. But you and I both know that summers come with lots of bugs." Mandy thought a minute. "Maybe one of those patio heaters would work in winter, too, although I'm not sure you can close them in."

"A built-in fireplace? With a chimney?" Drew's brows lifted when she shook her head. "Why not?"

"They'd have to haul wood. That means steps and lifting. That will be difficult for a while. And you know Ben wouldn't ask any of the hands to do it," she added. "He's too proud to say he needs help."

"Now who's looking at the angles?" He quashed his disgruntled feelings that she'd shot down another of his ideas. But Mandy was right about this. "I get caught up in logistical stuff too easily. I forget about the person."

"Buying Ella that beautiful cowgirl hat in the exact shade of purple she loves was clearly thinking about the person." Mandy's smile made her eyes look darker, like emeralds that held secrets. "The purple cowboy boots were too much though," she chided. "They're gorgeous, but her feet are growing so fast now that she likely won't even get a year out of them."

"So she'll give them to some other kid and I'll buy her another pair," he said with a shrug.

"You won't be here." From the way she said it, he knew Mandy hated reminding him of that.

"Maybe I could—" Drew never finished because two cars drove into the yard and squealing children emerged, chanting "Happy Birthday" as they raced over to Ella, who proudly showed them her new bicycle. "Showtime." He rose, clapped his hat on his head, stepped down and then paused. "You okay here for a while?"

"Yes, thank you. If I need help, Trina's just inside," she said.

"Then it's time for me to get Oliver into that clown outfit." Drew snickered at her surprise. "You didn't know he used to do that at kids' parties to raise money for college?" He shook his head and added teasingly, "I thought you knew everything about everyone who worked here, Mandy."

I don't know everything about you anymore. I wish I did.

Drew repressed the wayward thought to focus on his

daughter and the five children she'd wanted to host for her birthday.

He'd left the bottom step when he heard Mandy murmur, "Focus on the beautiful things. Let go of what you can't have."

He headed for the bouncy house to check its moorings, wondering what Mandy couldn't have. If he knew, maybe he could get it for her.

That's not your responsibility. Anyway, you're no good at responsibility.

Drew really wished he was, because it was suddenly very important that Mandy, who continually worked to make the world right for others, was also happy. He wanted to hear her carefree laugh ring out, to see those shadows leave her eyes so she'd be unafraid to rush into life as she once had.

Frustrated by his thoughts, he ordered his brain to stop thinking about Mandy and their shared past.

Easier said than done.

"I'm exhausted," Drew muttered to Oliver as they watched Ella blow out the candles on her cake.

"They'll probably all be gone in about half an hour," Oliver encouraged. "You can last that long, old man." He peered at the cake. "Why'd you give her a cake that's a house?"

"Ella mentioned wanting a playhouse cake before she went to camp, so I made one just in case. When she came back, she couldn't make up her mind until I showed her what I'd done. Doesn't it look right?" he asked anxiously, hoping that his prayers and God's promise to be there when needed had come together in a cake his daughter would remember.

Drew knew he was taking baby steps in this whole trust thing.

"Looks amazing with those turrets and stairs and chimneys. Quite artistic." Oliver suddenly paused. "I am so dumb," he said, smacking his hand against his forehead. "That's what you were drawing plans for every time we had a break."

"Actually, I asked a local guy to build it for her," Drew explained. "I'm not a very good carpenter. I only hope they'll get it out here for her to see before I leave."

"When will that be?"

"Not sure yet. I should know more tomorrow, after I see Bonnie and Ben." The whisper of late afternoon wind ruffled Ella's hair as she huffed out the last candle.

"I want a he-uge piece, please, Trina," Ella sang out. "For Mama. 'Cause I love her the mostest." She blew her mom a kiss and caught the returning one.

Before the kids had come to the table, Drew had set up a lawn chair and a little table. Then he carried Mandy there. Now she sat in the shade, near the kids, watching everything and taking pictures with her phone.

"We always put pictures in our beautiful things book," Ella had explained to Drew earlier. "So we don't forget."

Would they put a picture of him in there, he wondered? Even if they did, he doubted Mandy would leave it there for very long. She'd changed since she'd hurt her foot. Though she'd always been friendly, encouraging and cooperative, Mandy now didn't give away her emotions as easily as she once had. She wasn't sharing her thoughts either.

Even weeding Bonnie's precious garden, which had taken hours Drew should have spent doing his own work and left him with a backache and zillions of insect bites, hadn't brought more than a polite thank-you from Mandy. Nor had getting the calves branded, something she'd worried over incessantly until he'd told her it was done. She'd readily thanked him, but it sounded too civil, too—dutiful?

A barrier lay between them, one she'd deliberately erected, one he wasn't sure how to get past.

"Here's your cake, Drew. An' some for Oliver." Ella held out two plates heaped with cake and ice cream. "I love you." She grinned at them before scampering back to the table.

"She'll love your playhouse, too," Oliver said as they sat on the grass and savored their treat.

"I hope so." Was it stupid to want Ella to have something permanent from him, so she wouldn't forget him?

"Ella's your daughter, isn't she?" Oliver smiled at his surprise. "I figured it out a while ago. You have a lot of the same mannerisms."

"Impossible." Drew glowered at him. "Six weeks ago Ella didn't even know I existed and vice versa."

"That look right there—that's what I'm talking about," Oliver said, highly amused. "Ella gets that same cranky face when she doesn't like something. Which doesn't seem to be often, I must admit. Your daughter is a sweetheart."

"Don't call her that!" Drew gulped when Oliver frowned at him. "It's true biologically, but—I don't have any claim to her," he blurted in a lowered voice. "I don't have that right. Mandy's raised Ella all by herself for six years."

"Because?"

"Because I told her I didn't want kids. Ever." Drew sighed. "Apparently I said it so frequently and with such vigor that she felt she couldn't tell me she was pregnant." He bit his lip before admitting, "Maybe it was better that way."

"Huh?" Oliver's nose wrinkled with distaste. "Better how?"

"I'm not the fatherly type, Ollie. I don't even have a home," he admitted, only now realizing how true that was. "I have an apartment in New York that I thought I could make into my home, but it's not happening. It's just a place to live."

"Because home is where the people you care about live."
Oliver peered at him. "And you do care about Mandy and
Ella, don't you, Drew?"

"Yes," he admitted slowly. "But not in the right way."

"What's the *right* way?" Oliver shook his head. "Caring in the Hollywood movie kind of way? The way you
see on those big screen stories about magically overcom-
ing all obstacles, surmounting all issues and becoming
soul mates?" He snorted his disgust. "That's so not reality. I think love has more to do with hard work than simply falling," he said then took a bite of cake.

"What do you mean work? I thought—" Drew stopped,
suddenly aware that he sounded stupid.

"I think of romantic love the way I think about loving
God." Oliver chuckled at Drew's surprise. "Listen, when
you become a child of God, you don't rest on your laurels
and wait for life to serve you, do you? Life isn't suddenly
a rose garden. There are still trials to go through and lessons you have to learn."

"You mean be responsible," Drew muttered.

"Responsible? No, that's not exactly what I meant." The
cowboy ate his cake as he mulled it over. "Lots of people
think love is about finding the right person."

Drew didn't get what he was aiming at, so he remained
silent.

"I think love isn't so much about finding as *being* the
right person. I mean, you love Mandy, but you can't control her."

"That's for sure—hey, I never said I loved Mandy."
Drew frowned at him.

"No, you didn't." Oliver's steady regard pinned Drew.
"As I was saying, we can't control other people. We can
only control ourselves, be the right person, the one God
meant for us to be."

"You sound like you've gone through this yourself."

Drew hid his surprise when Oliver nodded. "What happened?"

"I couldn't forgive the lady for something so she chose someone who could," he said quietly. "I thought love meant there shouldn't be any problems, that she should be perfect. Turns out she wasn't perfect, and I was too dumb to realize that I wasn't either. I expected love to be easy, not that I would have to work at changing myself."

"I'm sorry," Drew offered.

"Don't be. It was a life lesson I needed to learn." Oliver offered him a crooked smile. "If something is worth having, it's worth working for. As Shakespeare said, 'Love is not love which alters it when alteration finds, or bends with the remover to remove, o no! It is an ever fixed mark that looks on tempests and is never shaken.'" He laughed. "Or something like that."

"I didn't know you were into poetry," Drew said. "I have a feeling there's a lot about you that I don't know."

"Hey, I'm an open book." The cowboy grinned a wicked smile.

They ate their cake in silence until Oliver broke it, his voice now very serious.

"Listen, Drew. The easy stuff is never the best stuff. Think if Jesus had taken the easy way out and stayed with His Father. He didn't because He loved us. Love in action." Oliver gazed at the mountains. "*Falling* in love is easy. It doesn't take effort. Ella's going to fall in and out of love repeatedly."

"Hopefully not for a while," Drew growled, disliking the thought of her getting hurt.

"Sooner than you think," Oliver said. "But being in love and staying that way, the action of *loving*, that takes commitment, hard work and something my dad used to call stick-to-it-ive-ness. Love isn't for weaklings, Drew."

Was that what he was, a weakling?

As Drew went about his chores later, he thought about Oliver's words. He'd never considered that loving someone meant work, but the more he thought about Mandy in relation to his parents, the more he realized his friend was right.

Even with a bad foot rendering her almost immobile, she showed her love for his parents by organizing the renovation of their home. She'd shown it in that fruit basket she'd taken to the hospital, in her phone calls to Bonnie and Ben every night. Love glowed in the pictures she messaged his parents and her encouragement of Ella to text her grandparents. Mandy's way of loving was far more costly than her job at Hanging Hearts could ever reimburse.

Mandy went out of her way to care for their staff, too, insisting the schedule must give everyone a weekend off twice a month. If they were short of help, she filled the gap herself. Drew had learned from his men's group that Mandy was highly favored among their neighbors, too, because, like his parents, she saw their needs before anyone else and found a way to help.

Beside her, Drew felt like a slouch. What did he give his parents? Money. He'd paid for a few alterations here. As if that would show his love for them. Cold comfort. He'd done the same with his own daughter. Bought her boots, a dress, a playhouse. But he seldom spent time with her, learned her favorite games, her favorite food or what she wanted in her future.

I want a daddy.

Shame swelled within him. He knew what Ella wanted, but he wasn't willing be the father who cared about her. He said he didn't want to be responsible. Was that the real reason?

Mandy.

Oliver had claimed Drew loved Mandy. Oliver was right. But Drew was terrified of that. What if he admitted it and Mandy rejected him? What if she was too fed up with him to risk a future together? He would be on the outside again, not a part of the Double H, not a part of Mandy's world, and maybe not even a part of Ella's life.

He couldn't risk getting close to Mandy. But dare he risk it with Ella?

Chapter Thirteen

"You didn't have to come today, Mandy." It was the second time Drew had said it. "My parents would have understood."

Mandy scowled. As if she would intentionally stay away.

"I missed Father's Day and the Sunday after. I am not missing this visit, no matter how hard you try to dissuade me," she insisted tightly. "So please stop."

"Why do you an' Mama always argue, Drew?" Ella picked up on the discord between them, as usual. "I don't like it."

"I wasn't exactly arguing, Bella Ella…"

Mandy huffed a sigh of relief when Drew let it go.

"We won't argue today," she promised with a severe glance at him.

Since the day after Ella's birthday two weeks ago, Mandy felt a rift building between Drew and herself. It was her own fault. She'd decided she couldn't keep letting herself be hurt by hoping for things—love and forgiveness—that she knew Drew would never give her. But he also seemed more withdrawn, focused on something he was mentally working through, though he hadn't shared what that could be.

"Do you think Uncle Ben will like my picture?" Ella's voice remained as subdued as it had been since she'd risen weeping on Father's Day, because God hadn't answered her prayer for a daddy.

"I'm sure Ben will love your picture, honey," Mandy said gently. Her daughter mourned the lack of a father every day, but there was nothing her mother could do to remedy that.

Knowing Drew would soon be out of her life and she'd be making this drive alone saddened Mandy. He'd stayed longer than she'd thought he would. She'd expected him to have left today. He probably would have if she'd totally been back on her feet. Well, that would happen tomorrow.

This time of being pampered and cared for had been wonderful, but it was growing too difficult for Mandy with Drew on the ranch, within sight and earshot all the time, never knowing when he'd stop by to visit Ella or for coffee, or to check up on her, bring a wildflower or a handful of wild strawberries he'd found on a ride. Each sweet occasion was tucked away in her heart, but they would make it so much harder to return to the solitary life she'd built.

There was no way around the truth. She loved Drew more than she ever had.

It was a mistake to let herself dream about sharing a future together. That kind of thinking made it worse because even if Drew somehow found a way to love her, that love would disintegrate when he learned the truth. And with each day that passed, Mandy grew more certain that she had to tell him. No matter what. She'd held back because she was afraid of his reaction, but also because of Ella. What would that revelation do to their relationship? For now Mandy took it day by day, preserving the facade of mere employee and boss's son but knowing it couldn't last.

"You said you need to leave the hospital early," he reminded her. "What's up?"

"My friends and I get together every so often to chat and keep up with each other. I've missed the last two meetings. I am not missing tonight's," Mandy insisted.

"But what about—?" He didn't need to finish that sentence. His glance at her ankle expressed his thoughts.

"I can drive to the coffee shop, walk inside and walk back out again without collapsing." She thrust out her chin. "I haven't used the crutch in days."

"Right." Drew's lack of argument surprised her, but then he'd seemed more introspective all week.

Several times while practicing climbing her front steps, she had noticed him and Oliver in serious conversation.

"We're here," he said, breaking into her thoughts.

Mandy carefully eased out of the car and walked into the hospital with her head held high. Nobody was going to see that her heart was breaking. Nobody was going to know how much she yearned to have this man love her *and* their daughter.

It was a relief to see Bonnie and Ben much improved since the last time Mandy had visited. Ben could still only manage a short walk because of his tender legs and feet, but he readily agreed when Drew offered his and Ella's services to push his wheelchair to the cafeteria so they could enjoy milkshakes together. Bonnie and Mandy chose tea and headed to the sunniest patch on the outdoor patio while Ella and the men chose a grassy knoll across the space.

"This is what I've missed most about being in the hospital." Bonnie lifted her face to the sun. "I'm sorry you've been stuck inside, too."

"I was, but I'll resume work tomorrow." Mandy smiled as if work was her only care.

"You'll take it easy at first, right?" Worry added tiny lines around Bonnie's eyes.

"Yes, ma'am. But I need to get back in the saddle, so to speak. Pun intended." She laughed at Bonnie's grimace.

"Drew has been amazingly helpful, and I'm very grateful to him, but he can't keep doing my job for me. He has his own career to look after. Anyway, my foot is much stronger. I have no more swelling and I'm tired of loafing around."

"It does get wearisome, doesn't it?" Bonnie's intense scrutiny missed nothing. "I've been praying for both you and Drew, Mandy, clinging to the scripture that God is an ever-present help in time of trouble." She peered across the patio where Ben and Drew were teasing Ella about her inability to whistle. "How are things between you?"

"Nothing has changed," Mandy said, then shook her head. "No, that's not totally true. Since Ella's birthday, Drew's been spending more time with her. In fact, he's the one who helped her get comfortable on the bike I gave her for her birthday. She was reluctant to get back on after a fall, but he's been diligent about convincing her that she's tough enough to master her bike."

"How amazing." Bonnie looked shocked. "I've been praying, of course, but I never imagined—Drew's always been so reserved and never related to kids at all…" Her voice dropped. "Thank you, Lord."

"He's been very good for Ella." Mandy smiled. "Everything she says lately is Drew this and Drew that. She challenges him if he doesn't give her a straight answer or tries to put her off. I doubt I'll get away with as much anymore."

"I'm so glad they're getting along." A single tear rolled down Bonnie's cheek. "He'll be leaving soon?"

"I think so." Mandy quashed a spear of pain. "I overheard him speaking to someone about a new job. I'm sure he wants to get back to New York and his numbers."

"Yes." Bonnie fell silent.

Mandy stared at her fingers, hoping to look nonchalant, unable to look directly at Bonnie because she would quickly discern that Mandy longed for Drew to stay.

"It was good of Drew to step in," she added. "But it's probably easier for him to work in New York."

"Not necessarily true." Drew's comment startled Mandy because she hadn't been paying attention as he'd left the others. He looked upset as his lips pinched together. "I can work anywhere. But don't worry, Mandy, I'll be leaving soon."

"I'm not worried—"

"Then you haven't found working at the ranch too cumbersome, son?" Bonnie interrupted.

"It's been remarkably easy for me to work from the Double H, Ma. Except for your internet." He smirked at her glowering expression and brushed her cheek with his lips before sitting. "I've been on time and on target with my projections for every contract so my clients are happy to pay my exorbitant fees."

"Such a shame we couldn't be there to enjoy your visit," Bonnie lamented.

"Don't worry, once you're back, I'll come home to make sure everything's okay," he told her. "We'll be able to share lots."

Mandy saw Bonnie's eyes light up at his use of the word *home*. She was surprised, too—he'd always insisted Hanging Hearts Ranch was not his home, never would be.

What had changed?

"I'm just sorry you had to give up so much of your time for us." Bonnie sighed.

"It's been good for me to be back." Drew grinned at Mandy's start of surprise. "I've made good friends in Oliver and some of the guys in my Thursday night group. At first they seemed to think I live a crazy life in New York."

"Don't you?" his mother teased.

"Hardly." He shrugged. "The more we share, the more we realize that all of us have issues, but what we're really after is quality of life. Being at Hanging Hearts has been a good time to figure out my priorities and what's most important to me."

And that is? Mandy didn't ask, but she sure wanted to.

"Look at that old man," Bonnie said fondly, her eyes on Ben, who was trying to make Ella's paper airplane fly. "When he's with her, it's as if he's twenty all over again."

"Ella's a blessing to all of us." Again, Drew's remark shocked Mandy.

He thought Ella was a blessing? Since when?

"The little sweetheart." Bonnie tipped her head to study him. "And God? Have you sorted that out, dear?"

"I'm working on it," Drew said very quietly.

"You don't have to 'work on' God's love, dear," Bonnie chided. "It's already been freely given. All you have to do is accept it and join His family." She sighed. "But you have to decide that for yourself, and it's a life-changing decision."

"Yeah." He studied his father and Ella for a few moments before his gaze slipped to Mandy. "I've been helping a couple of guys in our group resolve an issue between them. That's helping me realize that barriers we create aren't immoveable."

"I'm not sure I understand what you mean, son," Bonnie said with a frown.

"It means we all put up barriers because we're angry or scared or afraid. And the longer we leave them, the harder they are to take down."

Why was Drew looking at her when he said that? Mandy shifted uncomfortably. Could he possibly know…?

"I was just trying to tell you that this time I've spent on the ranch has been good for me, Ma." He patted her head, but a shriek of dismay from Ella had them all turning to see the problem. "Uh-oh. She's got her airplane stuck in that tree." Drew rose. "I'd better get back there before Pops tries to climb it." He left, chuckling.

"Sometimes God works in mysterious ways," Bonnie murmured.

Mandy was thinking the same thing. More specifically, that if Drew could face his barriers, so could she. It was time to tell him the truth and believe God would help her through whatever happened next, even if it meant leaving this wonderful couple and the place she thought of as home.

It was time to trust completely.

Drew wasn't sure what to make of Mandy's silence on the drive home. She barely answered Ella all through their fast-food dinner, staring out the side window as if fixated, and sniffing a couple of times as if she was crying.

When they arrived at the Double H, she hurried Ella inside with a brief thanks. He figured her meeting with her friends must be soon, but later, on his walk, he noticed her car was still in front of her house.

"Hey," he said when Mandy answered the door. "What about your meeting?"

"Trina's sick so Mama can't go," Ella explained.

Drew's brain kicked in. *My help cometh from the Lord. Help!*

"I'll stay with Ella." He held up a hand to stop her protest before it started, not exactly sure why he wanted to do this small thing to help her, except—he was the child's father! He should at least be able to manage a bedtime story. "I can do it, Mandy. Right, Ella?"

"Yep. Like I can ride my bike." His daughter grinned.

"You're sure?" Mandy's expression said she thought he'd lost his mind.

"I'm sure. Go."

"Okay." To his surprise she didn't argue, simply grabbed her bag and walked out, calling, "Text if you need me, Drew. Night, sweetie."

"Night, Mama." When the door closed, Ella studied him suspiciously. "Do you know about bedtimes?"

"I was kind of hoping you'd explain." He'd told Mandy he could do this. But doubt suddenly overwhelmed him until he remembered. *My help cometh from the Lord.*

"I already brushed my teeth and Mama combed my hair," Ella said. "An' I got my jammies on."

"So all you have to do is get into bed." A rush of relief filled Drew.

"No." Ella shook her head. "We gotta have stories first. I get one Bible story an' one other story. Sometimes two," she said, peeking through her lashes.

"Is that last part true?"

Ella sighed. "No," she admitted sorrowfully. "Come on. We sit in this chair. I sit on your knee." Once she had him arranged properly and had chosen the story, she handed him the children's Bible. "This one."

"Daniel in the lion's den." Drew had a hunch she had chosen it specifically. "Why this one?"

"'Cause sometimes I get a'scared," Ella said quietly. "When I hear about Daniel and how God shut the lions' mouths, then I feel better."

"I see." Drew read her the story slowly while wondering what his daughter feared.

"There." He closed the book. "You're safe here at the ranch, in your own house, with your mama, Ella. You know that. So why do you get scared?"

"'Cause sometimes bad stuff happens and I don't got a daddy." Her big brown eyes stared at him so innocently.

"But why do you need him when you've got your mom and Trina and Bonnie and Ben and all the people who work on the ranch?" he pressed, needing to understand.

"They're not my daddy." Ella frowned at him. "When your daddy wasn't there no more an' you came to live here, didn't you want your own daddy?"

"Yes, very much," he admitted, remembering how he'd longed for his former life.

"Why?" she asked.

"So he could see me, tell me stuff was all right, that I was a good boy and he was proud of me." Drew spoke from his heart, letting the old insecurities out of the cave where he'd kept them buried. "I guess I just wanted him with me."

"Me, too," Ella said, snuggling her head against his chest. "It's not 'cause I don't have a good mama. An' Trina and everybody's really nice. But..."

But. For all these years that had been Drew's issue, too. Ben and Bonnie loved him, *but* he'd wanted his own family back. *But* what if something he'd done or said had caused the accident? *But* if he let this place be home, was he somehow denying who he was and who his birth parents had been?

That night of the accident, Drew's parents hadn't heard him say he loved them because they were gone. But the truth was they'd known it, just as he'd always known they loved him. He'd let the shock of the accident and his insecurity build up and magnify inside until it tied him in fear, such deep fear that as a kid, he'd never gone to sleep at night without wondering if God would take his new family, too.

Yes, Drew had lost wonderful parents, but God had given him amazing people who had raised him with so much love. He saw now that no one had cut him out or excluded him. He'd made himself a loner, an outcast, by pushing away love.

And he was sick to death of trying to pretend he was still okay with that.

"I jus' want my daddy, Drew," Ella whispered.

The plaintive sadness in her yearning voice cracked the hard shell around his heart, finally freeing him to embrace the beautiful things he'd been given. Ella was one of those.

How could he have said he didn't want children? Ella was pure love. She'd become part of his heart. Drew couldn't bear to think he was causing her pain by denying her the one thing she needed to be completely happy and secure.

Yet the old doubts rose up anew. Maybe he'd be a lousy father. He'd probably do everything wrong. In fact, Drew's worst fear was that he'd fail his child. But he could not keep denying Ella. If he blew it, he'd just have to ask God to fix it.

As of this moment, he was finished with standing on the outskirts of life looking in. He would embrace love and whatever went with it. He would trust God as his help, fully, completely.

"Ella, honey, your daddy is right here. I'm your daddy, Ella," Drew whispered, tightening his arms around her.

"Really?" A flicker of doubt filled her brown eyes. "Really and truly, you're my daddy?"

"Forever," he promised.

Drew lost his breath as she threw her arms around his neck and repeated over and over, "I love you, Daddy. I love you."

"I love you, too, Ella."

She had a thousand questions and Drew had no clue how to answer most of them, but he was as honest as he could be.

"So you're my for-real daddy who loves me an' is gonna be with me forever an' ever?" she demanded when at last she wearily laid her head back on his shoulder.

"I don't know that part, sweetheart," he whispered, watching as her lashes drooped from tiredness. "I don't know what's going to happen tomorrow. All I know is that I love you very much, and whenever you need me, I'll be there."

"My very own daddy." She exhaled with a smile on her lips as sleep claimed her.

Drew kissed her forehead before rising to carry her to her bed. That was when he saw Mandy standing at the end of the sofa.

"You told her," she whispered, her beautiful face white and strained.

"Let me put her to bed and then I'll explain." Drew wasn't exactly sure how he was going to do that, so as he tucked his daughter in and brushed his fingertips against her satin cheek, he sent a plea for help heavenward. "You are the God of second chances. Please don't let me mess this up. Not again."

Then he returned to the living room to see how God would answer this prayer.

Mandy was not there.

Chapter Fourteen

Mandy sat behind Bonnie and Ben's house, beside the fire pit with the coals from the earlier youth group fire still glowing. She struggled to make sense of what she'd witnessed. Why would Drew tell Ella the truth now—unless he intended to take her away?

She slapped a hand over her mouth to stop her scream of denial. But her tears wouldn't stop.

"Mandy." Drew spoke from the gloom behind her. He stepped forward, uncertainty coloring his voice. "Hiding out?"

"Ella—" She jumped to her feet but Drew shook his head.

"Oliver couldn't come, but Miss Partridge will watch Ella until you return."

"You called her?" Mandy couldn't believe it.

"She stopped by with a late birthday gift for Ella... wait!" Drew must have known she intended to leave because he asked hurriedly, "Can we talk, Mandy? Or rather, can I talk?"

"I—I guess." *And say what?* she wondered as fear grabbed her throat. That he wanted his child? That she could never see Ella again? That she was a terrible mother?

Oh, why wouldn't these stupid tears stop?

"I should have waited to tell Ella until you were there, Mandy. I'm sorry," he apologized. "We'd read her story and she was telling me how much she wanted a daddy and why and, well, it hurt to hear her. Suddenly I just couldn't pretend anymore so I kind of blurted it out."

"Why now?" she asked, twisting her head to stare at him as he sat down beside her. "What's changed?"

"Me." Was that relief in Drew's voice? "I can't stand being on the outside anymore. I want into life."

"Huh?" She drew back when he burst out laughing, offended that he thought this was amusing. She rose to leave.

"Wait, Mandy, please." He still wore a silly grin. "It's just—I feel like I've lost twenty pounds."

"I hope not. You're already too skinny." Their familiar repartee from the past was back, and that made her burst into new tears. She flopped onto the bench and doubled over, sobbing her heart out. A second later Drew's warm hands curled around hers, drawing them away from her face.

"Stop crying, Manda Panda. I have something important to say and I need you to listen." He waited a fraction of a second before demanding, "Will you please look at me?"

It took every ounce of the little courage she had left to look at him hunkered down in front of her. "Well?" she prodded when he didn't speak.

"I love you, Mandy Brown. Always have, always will." He cupped her face in his palms, leaned forward and kissed away her tears. "There are a thousand reasons why and they'll take a lifetime to explain, but mostly I love you because you are the most remarkable woman I've ever known and you're the best mother our daughter could possibly have."

"You don't know—"

"Please let me finish." He smoothed her damp cheeks with his thumbs. "All those years ago, when I went off to college and you went to Missoula, I was scared. Whenever you called, you sounded so different, so distant. I was pretty sure you were regretting that time—well, I figured you were ashamed, and I was part of that shame. I thought you didn't want anything to do with me because of what we'd done."

"Huh?" Mandy couldn't believe this.

"The insecure kid who could never quite believe that God wouldn't take away his family again if he let himself love Bonnie and Ben became even more insecure when he left this ranch. I knew I loved you," he said emphatically, his warm minty breath bathing her face. "But I was scared to believe you loved me. So when you dumped me, I figured it was another one of God's tricks and I grew an even thicker protective shell around myself. I couldn't let anyone in."

She sat there, frozen, afraid to believe, to hope.

"I took me long enough, but I think I finally figured out something, Mandy." Drew smiled ruefully. "Love, which makes me vulnerable and terrifies me, is God's gift to me. Love can help me get through the hard parts of life, give me joy and companionship. If I let it."

Transfixed by his words and the smile that stretched to his dark eyes, Mandy sat in silence.

"That's what you do for me, Mandy." He brushed the tip of her nose with his forefinger. "You make my life better. I've never been more alive than when I'm with you. You are one of *my* beautiful things. And I love you more than I'll ever be able to tell you."

As Drew knelt in front of her, cradling her hands in his, Mandy knew this was what she had both longed for and feared.

"Will you please marry me so that maybe I can give you half as much joy as you give me?"

Delighted, shocked, afraid to believe he was serious, she burst into new tears.

"That was not supposed to make you cry." Drew's tortured expression hurt her heart. "Don't you love me? Have I been wrong to think…?" The words trailed away.

Mandy watched doubt fill him. She could have it all, the man she loved, life in the place she loved, a father for her daughter. Drew was offering her heart's desire. Everything she'd longed for was there for the taking.

If she kept her secret.

If she told the truth, he'd hate her and she'd have thrown away what she most wanted.

"Mandy?" His hands tightened on hers. "If Ella can trust God, can't we? Can't you trust me?"

And that was the bottom line. Either trust God to work it out or keep carrying her secret.

"Please, Drew, sit beside me." She studied his dear face and the confusion filling it. *Help me. I trust You, Lord.* "I need to tell you something."

Drew must have sensed her seriousness because he immediately moved to sit beside her. But he didn't let go of her hands.

"Whatever it is, it doesn't matter, Mandy. It won't change anything."

He didn't know, didn't understand. But he would soon.

"It matters. Just listen." She licked her lips and unlocked the secret box inside her that for so long had been filled with guilt. "Several months into my pregnancy with Ella, I learned I was having twins."

Drew's eyes widened.

"Simply being pregnant was mind-boggling, but knowing I was carrying two babies made it overwhelming. I didn't have much money. My insurance wasn't the greatest and I cut corners where I could, missed doctor's visits—so I could afford to eat," she added quickly lest he interrupt. "I was desperately scared about the future. I could barely wrap my mind around being a mother to one child, but two?"

Mandy stopped, engulfed in the past.

"Keep going," Drew encouraged.

"My faith wasn't the greatest then. I kept going over and over things, trying to figure out how *I'd* manage instead of leaving it to God. At night I had nightmares, so I didn't get much rest. I had to stop work because I couldn't be on my feet so much."

"If you would have told me—" His eyes widened. "Wait. I remember now. There was a call to the dorm once after we broke up."

She slowly nodded.

"I never called you back." He hung his head. "You'd dumped me and I was mad and I figured I'd make you wait until I came home for summer break."

"I know," she said quietly. "Please let me finish."

Drew nodded, his face sober.

"I got a little crazy as the pregnancy went on. I remembered how you'd always planned every detail, down to the nth degree, so I started planning, too."

"Planning what?" he asked, frowning.

"How I'd manage with two children." She licked her lips. This was almost the hardest part. "I considered adoption," she confessed.

Drew looked horrified.

"I was so scared. I thought that if a nurse or someone came for a visit after the babies were born, they'd see I didn't have proper clothes or a room for them and maybe they'd take one or both away from me." Mandy sighed. "I was trying to prepare by running scenarios, just like you used to do, but I just couldn't do that. Not with our children."

She studied her fingers wrapped around his, bracing herself.

"You must have been so worn out," he said softly.

"Very. The doctor kept telling me to relax, to take it easy, for the babies' sakes." She gulped. "I told myself to be strong for my babies. I tried. I went searching almost every day for work. Sometimes I got a few hours, but who wants to hire a hugely pregnant woman who can barely stand up straight? Nobody."

Mandy gulped and clung to his fingers, fearing this would be the last time she got close to Drew. He squeezed her fingers as if to encourage her to continue. He couldn't know how bad it would get.

"One day my landlady was sick. She offered me twenty dollars if I'd get her groceries for her. That was a lot of money to me, so I agreed. I was carrying them up the stairs of the building when I felt tremendous pain. I lost my balance on the stairs and fell. I passed out."

Drew's indrawn breath gave away his shock, but he said only, "Go on."

"I woke up in the hospital. They'd done an emergency C-section. One baby, Ella, was in the neonatal unit. They said she had breathing issues."

"And the other baby?" he whispered.

"Died." Tears rolled down her cheeks as she remembered and the guilt flooded in. "Because of me."

Mandy couldn't look at him. Couldn't see the loathing and disgust fill his face.

"I knew I shouldn't have lifted so much. It stressed the babies, which sent me into premature labor. Their heart rates were very high when I arrived, the doctor told me later. The other baby's heart wasn't strong enough. From what they said, I knew he might have survived if I'd taken it easy as I was told. He died because of me."

"He?" Drew's eyes met hers. "The other baby was a boy?"

"Your son," she whispered. "I'm so sorry, Drew. It was probably the stress that caused Ella's learning problems, too. I'm to blame for it—the mother who should have protected them both."

Drew said nothing. The silence was as forbidding as the look on his face. Mandy had to finish this.

"I have tried my best to be a good mother to Ella, but I'll understand if you want to take her away." The horrible words released, she wept anew.

"What?" Drew jumped to his feet, his face flushed. "I will never do that. Never, Mandy. How could you even think that?"

"But what if I mess up again—?"

"No!" He almost shouted the word. When she pulled back, he sighed, then knelt down in front of her once more and took her hands, his voice so tender. "Darling Mandy, please don't get into what-ifs. I've spent nearly seven years running from them. It's a quagmire you can never break free of. A dead end."

Darling? She stared at him.

"What I want more than anything, what I am asking you to accept, is marriage to me. I want us to be a family. That's my greatest desire." He freed one hand to touch her face and then followed it with his lips.

"But…" What Drew was saying—it didn't make sense to her. "But the baby. Your son."

"Your son, too." His sad eyes held hers. "I'm so sorry you had to go through that alone. I should have been there for you, taken care of you."

"You couldn't find me," she reminded him, bemused by his caresses.

"I should have. I was too self-involved. Shame on me." This time he kissed her properly, and Mandy kissed him back because she couldn't help it. "I love you, dearest Manda Panda. So much. And I think you're wrong, or perhaps you misunderstood the doctor because I don't believe you'd have done anything to knowingly endanger your children."

"I loved them both, but—"

"What did you name our son?" he asked, his forehead pressed to hers.

"Eric, in memory of the father you lost when you were nine." Mandy saw a single tear roll down his cheek and was aghast. "Drew?"

"Thank you, darling." He tenderly kissed her, then smiled into her eyes. "You know, I think my other dad has been looking after his namesake all these years we've been apart. But we're together from now on, right?"

"How can you trust me?" Shame filled her and she tried to break away, but Drew held her fast.

"Do you truly believe God is good, Mandy?" His gaze brimmed with love.

"Of course."

"Don't you think that God knew you'd fall, that Eric would die and Ella would have some problems? God knew it all and He trusted you to be the mother of a very special little girl. He gave you the knowledge and understanding to help Ella grow to be the most giving, sweetest child. He gave you love. Because that's what God is."

"I can't believe you're saying this," she whispered, her fingers clinging to his.

"It's about time I learned the lesson God has tried to teach me for so many years." A wry grin curved his lips. "I finally get it. If I want to belong, I have to make the effort. Nobody else can make me fit in. I have to let go of my fear and embrace the rough parts with God as my help. I have to let others help me heal and then help them. That's belonging."

"Yes," she whispered, delighted by his words.

"That's what I could never do after my parents died. I was too afraid of losing everything. I almost did anyway." He shook his head. "My stubbornness cost me a lot, especially you and Ella. All because I was afraid being vulnerable to love was some onerous responsibility, instead of the greatest privilege."

"So coming back to Hanging Hearts Ranch was a beautiful thing," she murmured, loving his smile.

"Absolutely. I finally realized God's love is waiting to be accepted. He'll tell me what to do if I will only listen. The ranch wasn't my home because I wouldn't let it be. But I belong now. Put that in your 'don't miss the beautiful things' book. Along with our wedding photo. Because you are going to marry me, right?"

"If you're sure you can forgive me?" she whispered soberly, searching his face for a trace of doubt.

"Can you forgive me, Mandy? For the past, which is a big ask, but also for the many mistakes I'll make in the years to come. I'm still learning, but I can promise you I will always be your loving husband and the very best father I can be to Ella."

"According to Ella, 'God forgived me, so I hafta forgive you.'" Mandy chuckled as Drew tugged her into his arms and began kissing her.

She had no problem returning his affection.

Epilogue

On the morning of her late September wedding, Mandy embraced her soon-to-be mother-in-law.

"I'm so glad you and Ben are back." Mandy's heart brimmed with thankfulness for the beauty in her life.

"Sweetie, if it gets us a brand-new daughter and a grandchild, we should leave home more often," Bonnie teased as she fastened the top button on her former wedding dress. "I never thought this would get used again but it fits you perfectly."

"It's the most beautiful outfit I've ever had. Thank you for loaning it to me," Mandy said as she gazed at her reflection.

"Just be as happy in your marriage as I have been," Bonnie ordered.

The ivory suit with its crocheted waist-length jacket and a long narrow crocheted skirt looked perfect with the short ivory boots Mandy had chosen. Her veil was a gift from Drew, an ivory lace Stetson.

"After all, you are the foreman of Hanging Hearts Ranch," he'd said yesterday after she'd thanked him. "You should look like it, especially on your wedding day."

"You're sure you don't want my job?" she said, only half teasing.

"Nope. I love my work. I'll help out whenever you need me, my darling, but numbers have always been my favorite thing. Second, no, third favorite," he corrected with a wink at Ella.

They'd deliberately made their wedding an informal occasion. Anyone who wished to come was welcome, which meant most of Sunshine was in attendance.

With white chairs arranged on the grass and guests waiting, Mandy paused a moment to study her groom, who stood patiently waiting for her, framed by the background of the snowcapped Rockies. Drew looked so handsome in his black suit with a red rose boutonniere that matched her bouquet. He would always own her heart. Beside him, Oliver waited, grinning as if he'd arranged the whole event.

"Can I go now, Mama?"

True to his word, Drew had bought his daughter a brand-new dress, a beautiful blue one she'd pronounced perfect with matching blue ribbons for her hair.

When Mandy nodded, Ella turned to her father and called, "I'm comin', Daddy!"

Laughter echoed into the mountains as she began walking toward Drew, scattering rose petals along the way. Trina waited for Mandy's nod, then stepped forward, elegant in her navy sheath. She stood opposite Oliver. Then it was Mandy's turn.

Drew caught her hand when she arrived, leaned forward and whispered, "You are so beautiful, Manda Panda."

"So are you," she replied.

"I'm not too skinny?" he asked with a wink.

"You're perfect for me." Mandy cupped her hand against his damaged cheek, knowing they would spend their lifetimes laughing and sharing and trusting their heavenly father. "Just what God planned."

They'd wanted to involve Miss Partridge because she'd prayed for them for so long. So they'd offered her the task of organizing food for their guests. The spinster librarian had excelled beyond their wildest dreams with a barbecue unlike anything Hanging Hearts Ranch had ever experienced.

"God never fails His children," she said when they thanked her before preparing to leave on their honeymoon.

"He does not." Drew bent and kissed her cheek. "You are a heaven-sent wonder, Miss Partridge."

"Oh! Cowboys are such flatterers." She left, giggling like a teenager, one hand holding her cheek.

"I want that recorded in your beautiful things book, Manda Panda. I have never seen Miss Partridge giggle before, or at a loss for words." Drew shared a secret smile with her.

"That's what happiness does," Mandy agreed.

"Everyone ready?" Oliver and Trina stood waiting at the car, ready to drive Mandy and Drew to Missoula, where they had a special surprise for Ella. Then the two friends would return to the ranch with Ella after delivering the couple to the airport to fly away on their honeymoon.

"We're ready." Mandy turned and tossed her bouquet, pleased to see that it landed in Trina's arms. "Perfect," she whispered to her new husband who looked puzzled. "There might be another wedding in the offing."

"Oh." Drew grinned, then called, "My ladies are ready so let's go, Ollie."

The mountain sun set earlier in September, so by the time Drew, Mandy and Ella had arrived at their secret spot, the last rays of daylight were waning.

"How come Oliver and Trina din't come?" Ella asked.

"Because we wanted some special time for just our family." Drew wrapped his arm around Mandy's waist and took Ella's hand. "Let's go for a little walk and then we want to tell you a story, Bella Ella."

"Okay." She danced along beside them until Drew stopped her.

"Can you read that?" he asked, squatting beside a head-stone.

Surprised, Mandy leaned in to read it, too, wondering when he'd had time to do this.

"It says, Eric Calhoun, our pre—"

"Precious," Drew coaxed.

"Precious son. Safe in God's arms. Love, Mama and Daddy." Ella twisted to study Drew. "You got the same name. Calhoun."

"Yes. And that's going to be your name, too, Ella," Drew explained, his hand finding and squeezing Mandy's.

"How come?" Ella wondered.

"Because I'm your daddy and because your mama and I got married so we could all be a family. Calhoun is your mama's name now, and we want it to be yours, too."

"Who's Eric?" Ella asked.

Drew couldn't speak so Mandy stepped in.

"Eric was your brother, honey. You were twins," she explained, trying to stop her tears as Drew's hand clasped hers. What a special man she'd married. "When Eric was born, he was sick and he died."

"We wanted you to know about him because he's part of our family, too." Drew smiled at Mandy. "And we don't want our family to have secrets from each other."

"Oh." Ella studied the headstone for a few moments more before asking, "So is my brother playing with Blackie now?"

"Probably," Mandy agreed.

"Cool." Ella considered that, then looked at her parents with curious eyes. "Can I get another brother to play with? An' maybe a sister, too?"

Mandy looked at Drew and gulped, thrilled by the prospect of building their family.

"We'll see," she said, resorting to her familiar response.

"I'm gonna ask God," Ella said.

"And you know how He answers her prayers." Drew grinned at Mandy's blush, hoisted his daughter to his shoulders, wove his arm around Mandy's waist and led them to the car. "This day for sure has to go in the beautiful things book."

This day, and all the rest they'd share.

* * * * *

If you enjoyed this story, pick up these other stories from Lois Richer:

A Dad for Her Twins
Rancher Daddy
Gift-Wrapped Family
Accidental Dad
Meant-To-Be Baby
Mistletoe Twins
Rocky Mountain Daddy
Rocky Mountain Memories

Available now from Love Inspired!

Find more great reads at www.LoveInspired.com.

Dear Reader,

Welcome to the first book in my newest ranch series set just outside Glacier National Park in Montana. I hope you've enjoyed Drew and Mandy's story and their journey to find that real love begins with our Father in heaven. Trusting in Him is a sure way to the find the beautiful things in life that He never meant for us to miss. I hope you'll join me in upcoming months for two more Calhoun brothers' stories.

I'd love to hear from you. You can write to me through Love Inspired publisher, at Box 639, Nipawin, Sask., Canada S0E IE0, or via email at loisricher@gmail.com. Or check me out on Facebook. I'll respond as quickly as I can.

Until we meet again, I wish you joy, love and peace as you uncover the many blessings God sends your way.

Blessings,
Lois Richer

COMING NEXT MONTH FROM
Love Inspired

Available April 21, 2020

A SUMMER AMISH COURTSHIP
by Emma Miller
With her son's misbehavior interrupting classes, Amish widow Abigail Stoltz must join forces with the schoolmaster, Ethan Miller. But as Ethan tutors little Jamie, Abigail can't help but feel drawn to him...even as her son tries to push them apart. Can they find a way to become a forever family?

AMISH RECKONING
by Jocelyn McClay
A new client is just what Gail Lapp's horse transportation business needs to survive. But as the single mom works with Amish horse trader Samuel Schrock, she's pulled back into the world she left behind. And returning to her Amish life isn't possible if she wants to keep her secrets...

THE PRODIGAL COWBOY
Mercy Ranch • by Brenda Minton
After their daughter's adoptive mom passes away and names Colt West and Holly Carter as guardians, Colt's determined to show Holly he isn't the unreliable bachelor she once knew. But as they care for their little girl together, can the cowboy prove he'd make the perfect father...and husband?

HER HIDDEN HOPE
Colorado Grooms • by Jill Lynn
Intent on reopening a local bed-and-breakfast, Addie Ricci sank all her savings into the project—and now the single mother's in over her head. But her high school sweetheart's back in town and happy to lend a hand. Will Addie's long-kept secret stand in the way of their second chance?

WINNING BACK HER HEART
Wander Canyon • by Allie Pleiter
When his ex-girlfriend returns to town and hires him to overhaul her family's general store, contractor Bo Carter's determined to keep an emotional distance. But to convince her old boss she's home for good, Toni Redding needs another favor—a pretend romance. Can they keep their fake love from turning real?

AN ALASKAN TWIN SURPRISE
Home to Owl Creek • by Belle Calhoune
The last person Gabriel Lawson expects to find in town is Rachel Marshall—especially with twin toddlers in tow. Gabriel refuses to risk his heart again on the woman who once left him at the altar years ago. But can they overcome their past to consider a future?

LOOK FOR THESE AND OTHER LOVE INSPIRED BOOKS WHEREVER BOOKS ARE SOLD, INCLUDING MOST BOOKSTORES, SUPERMARKETS, DISCOUNT STORES AND DRUGSTORES.

LICNM0420

Addie kept monopolizing Evan's time. First at the B and B—though she could hardly blame herself for that. He was the one who'd insisted on helping her out. And now again at church. Surely he had better places to be than with her.

"Do you need to go?" she asked Evan. "Sorry I kept you so long."

"I'm not in a rush. I might pop out to Wilder Ranch for lunch with Jace and Mackenzie. After that I have to…" Evan groaned.

"Run into a burning building? Perform brain surgery? Teach a sewing class?"

Humor momentarily flashed across his features. "Go to a meeting for Old Westbend Weekend."

What? So much for some Evan-free time to pull herself back together. "I'm going to that, but I didn't realize you were. The B and B is one of the sponsors for the weekend." Addie had used her entire limited advertising budget for the three-day event.

"I thought my brother might block for me today. Instead he totally kicked me under the bus as it roared by. He caught Bill's attention and volunteered me for the hero thing." The pure torment on Evan's face was almost comical. "I want to back out of it, but Bill played the 'it's for the kids' card, and now I think I'm trapped."

"Look, Mommy!" Sawyer ran over to them. A grubby, slimy—and very dead—worm rested in the palm of his hand.

"Ew."

At her disgust, Sawyer showed the prize to Evan. "Good find. He looks like he's dead, though, so you'd better give him a proper burial."

"Yeah!" Sawyer hurried over to the patch of dirt. He plopped the worm onto the sidewalk and told it to "stay" just like he would Belay. That made both of them laugh. Then he used one of the sticks as a shovel and began digging a hole.

"He's like a cat, always bringing me dead animals as gifts. I'm surprised he doesn't leave them for me on the doorstep."

Evan chuckled while waving toward the parking lot. She turned to see his brother and Mackenzie walking to their vehicle.

"Do you guys want to come out to Wilder Ranch for lunch? I'm sure they wouldn't mind two more. It's a happy sort of chaos there with all of the kids."

Addie's heart constricted at the offer. No doubt Sawyer would love it. She wanted exactly what Evan was offering, but all of that was off-limits for her. She couldn't allow herself any more access into Evan's world or vice versa.

"We can't, but thanks. I've got to get Sawyer down for a nap." Addie wasn't about to attempt attending a meeting with a tired Sawyer, and she didn't have anywhere else in town for him to go.

Evan's face morphed from relaxed to taut, but he didn't press further. "Right. Okay. I guess I'll see you later then." After saying goodbye to Sawyer, he caught up with Jace and Mackenzie in the parking lot.

A momentary flash of loss ached in Addie's chest. A few days in Evan's presence and he was already showing her how different things could have been. It was like there was a life out there that she'd missed by taking the wrong path. It was shiny and warm and so, so out of reach.

And the worst of it was, until Evan, she hadn't realized just how much she was missing.

Don't miss
Her Hidden Hope *by Jill Lynn,*
available May 2020 wherever
Love Inspired *books and ebooks are sold.*

LoveInspired.com